Ours for Halloween

Violet Taylor

Content Warnings

Ours for Halloween is a dark romance containing graphic violence and sexually explicit content that some readers my find disturbing. For a full list of content warnings, visit www.violettaylorauthor.com

To those who spend their days wishing for Halloween and their nights dreaming of monsters between their thighs...

Chapter 1
Evie

There are pumpkin guts on my shoe. A singsong array of "Trick or Treats" muffles the soft smush of pulpy flesh as I scrape the sole of my boot against the corner of the curb. The remnants of a carefully carved jack-o-lantern stare up at me. Another victim of a Halloween prankster. What's the point in smashing pumpkins? I wouldn't be caught dead disrespecting Halloween in such a manner. On years when there's a cold snap in November, any pumpkins I purchase get to decorate my front yard for as long as they like. The first freeze slows down their decomposition. Once Christmas rolls around, I just stick a skeleton in a Santa hat out there and claim it's Nightmare Before Christmas themed. That buys me some time. Last year, my perfectly placed pumpkin patch lasted until January before the weather warmed up and they turned into goo.

Halloween year round. That's always been my motto.

All Hallows' Eve is in full swing. Excitement twists within me like a spool of freshly spun webs. Halloween has always been my favorite time of year. Cool October air nips at my shoulders as it breezes past. The autumn chill I so often crave throughout the year settles into my bones, mocking my choice of wardrobe. Walking to the party seemed like a great idea at the time. My thoughts were more on fun and less on function when I slipped into the thin, lacy nightdress.

I think the outfit is spot-on. Of course, anyone without an obsession with Buffy the Vampire Slayer will probably miss the nuanced details that give away my Drusilla costume. Plus, I couldn't get those damn do-it-yourself fangs to work. I followed the instructions, but they just kept falling out of my mouth. So instead of a gorgeous Victorian vampire, I look like I've just run out of the bed of my rich, elderly husband after he died of mysterious causes. At least I have Drusilla's long dark hair and crystal-blue eyes. That will have to be enough.

Why am I so concerned with my costume anyways? I'm late as hell to this party. This particular group starts drinking when the sun goes down. By the time I get there they'll all be too drunk to care what I'm wearing. If they don't care, why should I?

A woman pushing a baby carriage strolls past, giving me a disapproving stare. I tug at the revealing dress self-consciously. More alcohol will solve this problem. The more I drink, the less I'll care. I pull the half pint of bourbon from the top of my boot and take a hefty swig. The smoky liquid coasts along my throat like friendly fire. It goes down surprisingly smooth, allowing me to finish it by the time I hit the next block.

My solo walk creeps on, giving me far too much time alone with my thoughts. Why did I think this was a good idea? Maddie hosts this party every year which means everyone from our very small circle of friends will be there. Everyone. Including my asshole ex, and his trash-bag friends. It's the downside to choosing a college in the small town you grew up in. There's no escaping the same people you've already spent your entire youth with.

I had the chance to leave, but pressure from my family and friends kept me close by. After graduation it just didn't make sense to go anywhere else. But every day that passes in this monotonous town brings me closer and closer to jumping in my car and driving into the sunset with nothing but the clothes on my back and the money in my pocket. That way I would never have to run into Sean again.

I wonder who he'll be tonight. The drunk, dribbling ex who is "still in love with me," or the douche canoe who goes out of his way to make my night hell and then hooks up with one of my friends just to prove he can control the group in a way I never will. On top of that, he's got all the other guys in our group scared into thinking he'll cut off their balls if they touch me. Which means I won't be getting any tonight. Looks like it will be another smutty book and solo adventure for me. Wait, did I put my vibrator on charge?

I'm pretty sure the answer is no. How depressing. A lame party, with unpredictable idiots, and no chance for dick? This night was doomed from the start.

The more I run through all the scenarios, the more I realize it was a horrible idea. And why the hell is it taking so long to get there? I've been walking for half an hour. It's getting unbearably cold, and my liquor bottle ran dry ten minutes into my journey.

I stop at the next street corner, working to get my bearings. I'm pretty sure it was a left on Bullard and then the second right onto Howard Way. Which I now realize should have been several streets back. I'm lost. Which is irritatingly on point with this evening so far.

A quick gust of wind rattles through the few dead leaves still clinging to the branches of a towering oak that looms above me. The sound reminds me of laughter. Even the trees are mocking me tonight. I drop my head, resigning myself to a well-deserved moping session. I'm only seconds into said session when my instincts bloom to life. The prickle of something that cannot be ignored slithers along the back of my neck and my pulse quickens.

Someone is watching me.

The revelation douses my liquor-warmed veins with ice water. I still, listening, looking. My gaze sweeps across the street, landing on a lone figure. The man that stands beneath a flickering streetlight is most definitely staring in my direction. His face is covered by a mask, but it doesn't matter. I can feel his eyes on me. It elicits a taboo rush that clambers to life in my gut. This part of the neighborhood is quiet and covered in a settling darkness that seems to have muted any sounds from the surrounding area.

I hold his gaze, uncertain of what I want to do. Or what I want him to do. Instead of doing the sensible thing, like looking for other people nearby or confronting this man for wigging me out, I turn. The thrill of giving him my back has my heart pumping and mind churning. Scenes from *Scream* and *Halloween* pique the interest of the mask-loving part of me that usually lies dormant between my thighs. There's clearly something wrong with me. A chastising tide of thoughts hovers above me, working to remind me of the proprietary nature that women are meant to uphold. But I've spent too many nights alone in the dark, drawing up fantasies that I'll never confide to any man. Maybe that's why I'm so keen to let something so foolish play out tonight. After all, it's Halloween.

I choose my next turn at random, picking a street with more darkened doorways than porches lit with jack-o-lanterns. My footsteps are steady, unassuming. I make it nearly to the end of the street before my curiosity bests my desire to appear nonchalant. One sweep of my long hair helps to hide my face as I peer over one shoulder. He's there, following behind me about half a street back. His pace is even but determined. His strides measured. The red mask is dark, demonic, and only manages to increase the swarm of butterflies currently fighting the bourbon for space in my stomach.

How long can I play this game? I guess I'll play as long as he continues to follow me. Or until he makes a move. A sudden twinge of disappointment rips me loose from my excited fantasies. What if it's someone I already know beneath those monstrous features? It could be one of Sean's friends sent to torment me. My thoughts circle back to the masked stranger's build. He's tall, broad, and built in a way that screams *not from around here*. The best we've got are ex-football players whose high school dreams have already dwindled into desk jobs. The guy in the mask most certainly didn't end up shaped that way from sitting in a cubicle eight hours a day. I can tell by the way he walks, or really stalks, behind me.

The screeching of tires draws my gaze over my shoulder once more. Some idiot in a rusty red Bronco rushes past my masked man, swerving all over the road. "Don't drink and drive, kids," I mutter as I edge out of the street and onto a sidewalk.

"Aren't you a pretty little thing." The car slows next to me. "You need a ride somewhere?" His words are slurred.

"No thanks," I offer with barely a glance his way. I worked in a dive bar all through college. I'm used to creeps.

"Come on, sugar. I've got something real fun planned for tonight. Why don't you get in the car? It's cold out here." I ignore him. With any luck he'll get bored and drive off. "I'm talking real nice to ya. So why don't you just hop in—"

"Fuck off." I stop walking and turn the full intensity of my best bitch stare his way. My spine straightens as I take in the man staring back at me. Have you ever looked at someone and just known there is something off? It's the eyes. Like when you go to the zoo. You can always tell which ones were born there, and which ones once lived without a cage. There's something about the eyes. A wildness. An unhinged darkness that stares back at you through a gaze that's vacant of empathy and joy. An icy detachment that supersedes unspeakable evil. That is what I see reflected in the murky brown eyes of the weathered man before me. Evil.

I take off running. My thoughts turn to the masked man. Is he close? Will he help me if this man tries to take me by force? The screech of tires sounds, followed by a loud crash as he nails the curb to my right. I glance back, but cannot see any sign of the masked stranger.

My legs are burning. I'm just a few feet away from the next cross street. My heart lurches into my throat as I hear the car reverse. The driver guns it once again, drawing my attention behind me. But this time the car is close. Too close. *He's coming right at me.* Headlights blind me seconds before impact.

My body slams to the ground hard enough to steal the air from my lungs. It's an unwelcome sensation I haven't experienced since childhood, when I fell from the monkey bars in the backyard of the house I grew up in and landed flat on my back. The air shot from my lungs, not returning for what felt like minutes, but was probably only seconds. As an adult, the experience is far more traumatic.

My eyes flick open, but instead of a bumper, I find a red Halloween mask. I open my mouth to scream but the air still hasn't returned to my lungs. The man rips the mask off, revealing amber eyes and shaggy blond hair.

"I've got you. Calm down. I'm here with you." His voice runs through me like melted molasses and something warm and calm washes over me. I still can't fucking breathe. His massive body has me pinned to the ground. Did he push me out of the way? Tires peel out as the driver vacates the scene. That asshole almost killed me. I lift up my arms to shove the very large, very heavy man currently lying on top of me away but the damn things won't move. My arms, my legs, my lungs. Nothing is working.

The fear in my wild eyes is reflected in the soft honeyed glow of the stranger's gaze. His eyebrows are furrowed, his jaw set in a grimace. Why is he looking at me like that? Am I wounded? Did I get hit after all? Are my guts spilled out like a smashed pumpkin across the perfectly manicured lawn I'm sprawled out on?

"I've got you," he keeps saying. *Yeah, no shit you've got me. You're literally crushing me.* I want to scream at him to move, but nothing happens. The seconds tick by and he continues to murmur in my ear. "I've got you. You're safe now. Calm down."

And eventually I do.

There's something about his voice. His words weave around me like an embrace. I suck my first breath in, in what feels like a lifetime, and his face brightens. "There she is."

"Get off me." I lift my arms which are finally obeying my commands and shove at his chest.

"Sorry." He sinks back on his feet before standing. "Are you hurt? Can you stand?" He offers me a massive, callused hand. I take it on instinct. His skin is overly hot beneath my fingers.

"I think I'm okay. You were just crushing me. But thank you, for knocking me out of the way. I thought I was a goner." He pulls me to my feet and I take a rushed breath in. My face comes up to the middle of his chest. He's well over six feet. I crane my head back, my gaze running up the length of his lean neck and sharp jaw until it meets those twin amber irises. *Were they glowing so brightly before?* My hand is still clutched in his grasp. His fingers pulse with warmth against my chilled skin. He gives me a lazy half grin that has me flushed and fumbling. I take a quick step back, putting space between us. His smile drops and he gives me the strangest look.

"Your eyes..." I start, noting the way they've brightened even more. His brilliant eyes widen and quickly snap back to the spot where his mask is lying on the lawn. He snatches it up, sliding it over his face and blocking his beautiful, rugged features. I can't deny my disappointment.

It does give me a chance to study the mask more closely. It's wooden, and painted with various shades of red. Two curved horns jut out into the dark sky above. They lead down to an oval pair of pupilless eyes. A man's nose sits just above a monster's mouth. The jaw is long and wide, with sharp teeth carved into the wood. The mask is completed with an over-the-top tongue that twists out of the gaping jaw and stretches several inches farther than a natural tongue can go. I've never seen such a mask. I wonder if he carved it himself.

"What's your name?" There it is again. That warm, masculine voice. My eyes drop toward his mouth, wanting to see the words formulating on his sharp, shapely lips. I find only the wooden jaw of the Halloween mask.

"I'm Evie."

"Evie." The word comes out soft and wanting. "I'm Hess."

I can't help but pop an eyebrow. "Hess?"

He chuckles and the deep tone sends electricity down to my toes. "It's a nickname. Where are you headed, Evie?"

My body has an instant reaction to the way he says my name. "Just some friend's party. Which I'm starting to think was a horrible idea. Maybe almost getting run over was a sign that I should head home and have a quiet night in."

"A quiet night in? On Halloween? I can't allow it." Hess chuckles again. "Come to my party instead. I promise it will be better than wherever you were headed before."

"Your party?" A red warning light flashes in the depths of my mind.

"I'll even drive you to ensure you arrive safe and sound. Someone who looks as dangerously enticing as you shouldn't be out walking alone on a night like tonight." Heat pools in my cheeks. His mask tips down and back up as it runs the length of my body. I can't see his eyes and it's driving me crazy. The desire to rip off that mask and stare into his unusual gaze has my fingers twitching at my sides. His words bring me back to the unnerving man in the car. But Hess isn't giving me any of the frigid, terrified feelings the other man did. In fact, I feel safe and comfortable. Despite having just met him. He seems like a good guy. That, or this is trauma bonding at its finest.

When I don't answer right away, he adds, "I'll make sure you don't get bothered by any more creeps tonight. You have my word."

"Is it far?"

"Not far at all. We're down by the Old Mill ruins."

"I heard that place is haunted," I tease. The Old Mill ruins run along a roaring creek hidden just within the woods. People flock to it on hot summer days and families splash around in its cool, shallow depths. But when the sun goes down, everyone packs it up and heads out of the forest.

There are countless tales of ghosts among the trees and voices in the water. We used to go there as teenagers and sit in the dark. We would take turns venturing off alone until one of us got so scared we all ran full speed back to our cars. I haven't been down there in years.

"I'm scarier than anything haunting those woods," Hess says, his voice lacking any trace of humor. He holds out his hand. "You'll be safe with me."

You would think following a masked stranger to a party in the middle of the woods on Halloween night would trigger the part of my brain that's addicted to murder podcasts and cold-case files. But the voice within me that guides my actions and warns me when something isn't right is suspiciously quiet. Even with the faintest trickle of fear in the back of my mind, my curiosity drives me forward. My palm hovers over his, and his fingers close around me, burning with that same unusual heat.

Hess guides me down another street to where a shiny black truck is parked beneath another flickering streetlight. He opens the door like a gentleman, not dropping my hand until I'm tucked inside. His actions are charming and unexpected. But I can't deny the edge of danger that hovers around him like a lingering shadow.

My eyes are drawn to his hand on the steering wheel. The muscles in his forearm flex with each turn of the wheel. Prominent veins run along his hands and wrists. Hess is the definition of masculine. The force, weight, and firmness of his body against mine when he pushed me to the ground and nearly suffocated me made that achingly obvious.

My mind wanders to the other reasons he could have for pinning me down. The weight of him on top of me, with no clothes between us. His large hands exploring me. My body tingles with the visions of him taking me on the ground, forcing pleasure from my body beneath the pitch-black sky. Someone as large as he is must be proportionate in other areas...

"Careful, Evie. Your thoughts aren't nearly as well guarded as you think." His mask turns toward me. "And I'm trying to be a gentleman."

"I wasn't—" The truck slams to an abrupt stop. Hess faces me, draping his arm over the back of my seat and putting the full size of his broad chest on display.

"Do you want me here? Or can you stall those devious thoughts long enough to make it to the party?"

My mouth drops open. Shame sends flames flickering up my neck and into my cheeks. My words pour out in a stuttering mess. "That is... I can't believe... You just. Excuse me? We just met."

"So you weren't just imagining what it would be like to fuck me in the dirt?" I can practically hear the smile behind his words.

"How dare you? Please, don't be so fucking presumptuous." I twist away from him, folding my arms and praying my blush isn't as bright as it is hot.

"Dare? That's not a bad idea." He turns back to the wheel and begins driving again. I'm suddenly wishing I had a mask of my own. It's completely unfair that he gets to hide his emotions while mine are on full display. I can't help but think he finds this whole thing amusing. It's not as if he threatened to take advantage of me. No, he called *me* out for wanting to take advantage of *him*. God this is so embarrassing. Why am I always drawn to dangerous bad boys? And how the hell did he know what I was thinking?

The trick-or-treaters and streetlamps fade behind us as we move into the dark wilds of the Old Mill woods. The trees here are ancient. Their knotted branches reach up to the sky, twisted wooden fingers seeking to lure the moonbeams closer to their darkened pathways.

Hess pulls off the road, parking in a small clearing. He turns the truck off. The headlights vanish and we're swallowed up by the night. The spicy scents of cinnamon and cloves waft off him like fall itself. He turns to face me and I swear I can see the glow of his amber eyes through the small slits in his mask.

It's so quiet here. I become aware of my own breathing. In the silence that surrounds us, even the sounds of air slipping from between my lips seem overly loud. Hess's breathing is quiet, steady. My eyes trek along his torso, landing on the fitted red shirt. His lungs expand, pressing every muscle to the surface of the thin fabric.

"Evie?" His voice has my gaze shifting to the slits in his mask. "Are you ready?"

I take a moment to survey my surroundings. There are no other cars. Not a single sign of any other people out here. My throat sticks as I swallow. No one in their right mind would wander out into the dark forest with someone they just met. But I hunger for adventure and the thrill of the unknown. Somehow, I know with great certainty that Hess will be the one to feed those needs.

"Lead the way," I whisper, afraid to offend the silent beauty surrounding us in this moment.

Hess helps me out of the car, taking my hand in his and guiding me through the densely packed trees. The heat of his touch sinks into me, warming me to my soul.

"Most girls would have chosen Buffy. Why'd you choose Drusilla?" He doesn't look back when he speaks, just keeps leading us deeper into the forest.

"You recognize my costume?" I scoff in surprise.

Hess laughs, and the sound is deep and sinful and utterly satisfying to the part of me that's taking great pleasure in his presence. "I may be a bit of a Buffy fan."

"That's unexpected." I giggle.

"So tell me, why'd you choose Drusilla? Most people idolize the slayer." He ducks beneath a low-hanging branch, pulling me under after him.

"I guess I've always had a thing for monsters."

Hess stops walking so abruptly that I run straight into his back. He turns, peering down at me from beneath his mask. "Is that so?"

Our bodies are close enough that I can feel his heated skin through the lacy fabric of my nightgown. He lifts a large hand, tucking my hair behind my ear with surprising gentleness. My breath hitches as his fingers slide down, grazing my jaw. Goosebumps rise across my flesh everywhere his warm skin touches mine. His thumb brushes along my bottom lip and my mouth parts in response. My gaze drops to the wide mouth of the wooden mask. Plush, firm lips are just out of reach, guarded by the sharply carved teeth of a Halloween costume I'm quickly tiring of.

He leans close enough that the long wooden tongue nudges my chin. "Are you afraid of me?"

"No," I breathe out, tilting my chin closer to the mask.

Hess wraps his other hand around my waist, dragging me flush against him. "Maybe there's a little monster in you after all."

My hands slide up his muscular chest, moving ever closer to the base of the mask. I grip the edge, slipping my fingers beneath. A shrill scream has me jumping away from Hess and peering around. A woman's laughter quickly follows.

"We're nearly there, come on." Hess reaches for my hand and moves more quickly through the trees. The golden-orange glow of a bonfire exposes the well-hidden location of the party. We break through the tree line and enter a clearing that's nestled between the water and the stone ruins of the mill. There are a dozen or so men and roughly half as many women. Some lounge on fallen trees around the fire, while others sit on the wide, flat boulders that edge the creek. The atmosphere is cozy, thrumming with laughter and conversation. The girls are in costumes that range from conservative, to spooky, to lingerie and animal ears. The men are all dressed casually, each with a unique wooden mask obscuring their features.

"Hess is back!" a stocky man with an orange mask that depicts six eyes and two walrus—like tusks—yells out, raising his cup. The others turn, cheering and making toasts.

"You're popular," I mutter, suddenly uncomfortable with all eyes on us. Hess's hand stays firmly wrapped around mine.

He chuckles. "I kept them waiting long enough."

Two men who are similar in size and stature to Hess rise and make their way toward us from the other side of the bonfire. One is wearing a deep-green shirt with an even greener mask. The other is wearing black from head to toe.

As they move closer, an unexpected sensation flutters within me. My eyes devour the way they walk. Like predators. Their spines are straight and proud. There's something about the way they move. It's as sensual and dangerous as Hess.

"You made it. We were worried," the first man says, his green mask tilting down toward me.

"Evie, this is Luda." The green-masked man reaches his hand out to shake mine. I take it, feeling a blush ruddy my cheeks yet again. His arms are as thick and veiny as Hess's. I'm instantly dying to see beneath his mask.

"Nice to meet you," I respond politely.

"It's such a pleasure to meet you, Evie." There's a playful note to his voice. Luda draws my hand beneath his mask. The feel of cool lips on the inside of my wrist makes me shiver.

"And this is Reiner." Hess nods to the figure in the black mask. He reaches for my hand and I yelp as electricity sparks between us. He abruptly jerks his hand back, flexing it by his side.

"Woah, shocked me." I laugh, rubbing the inside of my palm with my thumb.

"Apologies, Evie." Reiner takes a step back, his voice tight.

Luda claps a hand across his shoulder. "Just a little static. Nothing to worry about, mate."

As I study them a moment longer, I recognize that their masks are almost identical to the one Hess is wearing. The only differences are in the colors and the size and shape of the horns.

"Can we get you a drink?" Luda offers.

"That'd be great. Thanks."

Luda heads to a nearby table and I see the faintest hints of white-blond hair beneath the strap of his mask.

"Let's get you warmed up." Hess wraps an arm around my shoulders, leading me to an empty space on a nearby log. I glance back to find Reiner still standing where we left him.

"Is he alright?" I nod his way. Hess sighs, turning to his friend.

"Reiner is... Well, I'll go check on him." He strolls casually away and my eyes drop to the impressive swell of his ass. Damn he's a hell of a specimen. A quick fluttering to the right of my face has me swatting the air.

"Calm down, honey. It's just a butterfly." A tall, beautiful girl in a short, blue wig and a shimmering silver bodysuit stumbles my way. The front of her costume is unzipped far enough to show off a generous amount of cleavage. "Shoo." She flaps a hand at it.

"Technically, it's a moth." Another girl approaches. She has glossy, red hair that covers half her face, giving her a sultry Jessica Rabbit look. One dramatic smoky eye with golden false lashes and a brilliant blue iris sparkles down at me.

Her outfit is what I can only assume is meant to be a Cupid costume. It consists of large, fluffy wings, a pink, feather-lined teddy, and a gold bow and arrow with hearts painted all over it. "A Death's-head moth, to be exact."

The large black and gold moth settles on my shoulder. Six fuzzy legs climb up my sleeve and two long feelers stretch out in front of it. It's beautiful in a dark, mesmerizing sort of way. With deeply colored wings and a small skull-like marking on the back of its head.

"They're all over this place." The blue-haired girl shudders dramatically. "I'm Georgia."

"Evie." I shake her hand, careful not to disturb the moth.

"You are just beautiful, Evie." Georgia has one of those endearing Southern twangs. She certainly isn't from around here.

"So are you." I smile back at her.

"Welcome to the party. It's moth central but the drinks are fabulous and the men..." Her eyes roam across the fire, landing on a shirtless man with his back to us. "Honey, let's just say there must be something in the water with this bunch."

"What was your name?" I turn to Cupid.

"Cami." She shakes my hand, revealing perfectly manicured, pink-tipped nails. "Who'd you come here with?"

"Hess." I search behind me, finding Hess still speaking to Reiner. "There. Red shirt."

"Damn girl, he is built." She fans herself theatrically.

"Are you two dating?" Georgia asks, taking a seat on the log beside me.

A rush of embarrassment fills me. "No. Uh, we just met. Some idiot actually tried to run me over. Hess knocked me out of the way. So when he invited me to the party, I couldn't exactly say no."

"That is so cute. He saved you. Kodi saved me too but not quite so literally. I climbed my ass to the top of the Ferris wheel during a dark moment of alcohol-induced insanity. He talked me out of jumping, carried me all the way down, and then brought me here! He's a real sweetheart." The apples of Georgia's cheeks round as she grins.

Georgia's story makes me think of another girl from several years back. She jumped to her death from the top of the Ferris wheel in some little town down south. It made national news. I wouldn't think suicide by Ferris wheel was a common choice, but I guess it happens more often than I thought.

Cami sits on Georgia's right, locking her arm with other woman. "Well I'm glad he talked you down and I'm glad Ethan took care of my psycho, stalking ex. We both ended up here and now we're instant besties. Plus, our dates are besties. It's perfect."

"Psycho, stalking ex? That sounds rather dramatic," I add with a smirk.

Cami sighs. "It was. He'd been following me around for months. I blocked his number and got a restraining order, but that psychopath still had the balls to confront me at the bar tonight and put a fucking gun to my face."

"Jesus," I mutter. My ex may have been a dick, but I'm pretty sure he would never pull a stunt like that.

"Ethan took him out before he could pull the trigger. With any luck, he's in a hospital somewhere with amnesia. It's going to be a mess to go to court if not, and I sooo don't want to deal with that," Cami whines, sticking her bottom lip out.

"We are not worrying about that tonight. Kodi, Cami is moping! We need more drinks!" Georgia calls out.

"Did someone say drinks?" Luda drops down in a crouch before us, passing around three Solo cups. "Shots for you, you—"

"Yes, you're an angel. Cheers! To losing our minds for one night and following a bunch of hunky strangers into the woods on Halloween." Georgia grins, taking a drink and shoving one in Cami's hand. I assumed the others were at least dating. Did we all meet our masked men tonight? My fingers brush Luda's as he passes me a cup. The touch of his skin is cool, smooth. I down the contents, grimacing as the heavy burn of some sort of strong rich liquor races down my throat.

"Jesus, was that a triple?" Cami coughs, dropping her empty cup to the ground.

The alcohol rushes through my body, filling me with warmth and a sudden airiness. I probably should have eaten something before diving straight into shots.

"What happened to Hess and Reiner?" I ask Luda. The two have not returned to the party and are no longer standing in the spot I last saw them.

"Not sure. I guess we better go find them."

I squeal in surprise as Luda scoops his massive arms beneath me, lifting me off the ground and hauling me to his chest.

"Oh my gosh." I giggle, feeling slightly embarrassed. Luda moves across the clearing with purposeful strides, his strong arms bearing my weight like it's nothing. I lean into his hold, thoroughly enjoying the feel of his muscles pressed against me. I peer up at his mask, my curiosity as to what his face looks like growing by the second. There's a salty scent to him, like an ocean breeze with a touch of something fresh and plant-like. He tilts his head down, and I can make out the slight glow of green beneath the slits of his mask. The fingers beneath my knees stroke softly, making me shiver.

"What did we miss?" Hess's baritone voice comes from my right. I turn my head and find him and Reiner moving out of a shadowy thicket of woods.

"Our little monster was missing you two," Luda says with what I know must be a smirk on his face. His energy is all golden retriever. It's far less dark and dangerous than Hess's *let me lure you to your death, it will be worth it* vibe. I haven't gotten a good read on Reiner yet. As of right now he's quiet, mysterious. The hint of shaggy raven hair peeks out from the sides of his mask. Luda sets me on the ground so that I'm standing between the three of them. How can they all be so fucking tall? They've got to be clearing six-three, maybe more.

"Is that so?" Hess drops his hidden amber gaze to me. Something about the way he focuses on me, even without being able to see his eyes clearly, makes my blood heat.

"What should we do now that we found them?" Luda asks from behind me, his fingers toying with a strand of my hair.

"I think Evie wanted to play a game earlier? Didn't you mention a dare?" Hess's words make me pray the shadows of the night are enough to hide my shocked expression. He's referring to the moment he called me out for daydreaming about screwing him. He's testing me, trying to see if I'll give the details of our conversation to the others. Instead of giving him the satisfaction of embarrassing me, I simply agree.

"Yeah, I thought a little game of truth or dare might be fun." I pull off the sentence with more confidence than I feel in the moment and give myself a mental pat on the back. Luda's touch in my hair stills.

Hess moves closer, his fingers brushing just beneath my chin. "I think that can be arranged." His hands drop to my waist, hugging it tightly. Before I have a moment to ready myself, I'm tossed over his shoulder. "Go on, Luda, round everyone up."

"Hess, put me down!" I call out in a halfhearted protest. This is the second time in the last few minutes that I've been manhandled and carried around like a damsel in distress. Honestly, I don't hate it. Both Luda and Hess are *strong*, strong. I've always been a sucker for an overly athletic build.

Hess gives me a smack on the ass that has me yelping in surprise. "Behave, little monster."

A rumbling chuckle comes from beneath Reiner's mask. He trails behind us, and I take the chance to study him. He's the broadest of the three. Where Luda's skin is soft and pale, and Hess's is a golden tan, Reiner's skin has a rich bronzed tone. His hands are buried in his pockets as he walks in silence.

Hess doesn't release me until we've reached the bonfire. But instead of setting me on my feet, he shifts my weight so that I end up on his lap. One arm wraps around my waist. The other accepts one of the drinks Luda is offering us. I'm acutely aware of Hess's body so close to mine. His fingertips graze my waist, his breath tickles my neck, and that delicious fall scent floats around me once more.

There are already a few couples sitting around the fire. All the women are in costumes. All the men are in masks. "Why are the three of you wearing the same masks when everyone else's are different?" I search the group for similarities. "Except those two." I spy a pair with identical masks. Other than that, each mask is completely unique.

"We all chose the mask that best fits us," Hess tells me. "The three of us have a lot in common, so we got similar masks."

That answer doesn't satisfy my thirst for knowledge in the slightest, but as Hess's hand drops from my waist to my thigh, I forget all about my questions and focus on the way my body is reacting to his touch. His fingers inch higher and dampness collects between my thighs. I'm ashamed such a simple touch can cause such an intense reaction. It's been way too long since I've had any attention in that department. If I'm not careful I'll leave a damn wet spot on his jeans.

Hess chuckles behind me. "And you think I wouldn't love it if you did?"

I choke on my drink mid-sip. Did I say something out loud? No, I'm certain those thoughts were unleashed strictly in my mind. There's no way he could know what I'm thinking. Of course, I could just ask him what he meant by that. I don't, though. What's stopping me? It's that nagging feeling deep inside that maybe he really does know what I'm thinking. If so, I sure as hell don't want him vocalizing those thoughts.

"Someone mentioned truth or dare?" A growly voice startles me as a large man in a wolfish mask drops into the seat beside Georgia. The others make their way to the fire. It's hard to tell for sure, but there are at least ten couples.

"Ooooh, I love this game. I want to go first." Georgia's eyes sparkle with mischief.

"Here we go." Cami giggles.

Georgia's gaze snaps to Cami. "Cami, truth or dare?"

"Me?" Cami protests. A towering figure in an elongated navy mask has an arm slung around her shoulder. I think she said his name was Ethan. His muscular body is enormous. I laugh to myself, imagining the look on the face of Cami's deranged ex when Ethan intervened and beat his ass. That's a fight I would have paid to see. Cami blushes slightly before answering. "Truth."

"Not an option," Georgia says.

Cami rolls her eyes. "Fine, dare."

"I dare you to give Ethan a lap dance." Georgia's gorgeous face is sporting a grin that's giving off major evil genius vibes.

"Absolutely not," Ethan snaps. "Look what she's wearing, she'll be exposed to the whole group." Cami's short pink teddy and heels combo is by far the most revealing costume here. Ethan's right. We'd be getting an eyeful of whatever's beneath her skirt the first time she bent forward.

"Fine." Georgia pouts. Her gaze coasts across the group, landing on a dark-haired girl wearing a slutty pirate costume. She's nestled in-between the two men with matching purple masks. "Sonja, give one of the twins a—"

The other woman's dark eyes widen before narrowing. "You didn't even ask me truth or dare."

"That's because I know someone as crazy as you ain't gonna pick truth, darlin'."

Sonja grins. "Very true. What's the dare?"

"Give one of the twins..." Georgia stops, her eyes lighting up. "Give *both* of the twins a lap dance, at the same time. Rhylan, Khenlyn, assume the position." She smiles triumphantly.

"If I must." Sonja tosses the group a wink before turning to the twins. She has them turn so that they're straddling the log, with one facing her and one behind. They scoot together close enough for their knees to overlap. Sonja drops down between them, rolling her hips and grinding so that one twin is getting the front of her writhing body, while the second gets her ass. The uneven fabric of her pirate dress rides up her thighs as she moves. The twins bend forward, their masks running along her neck as their hands explore her body.

"Damn, enough! I said a lap dance, not a three-way." Georgia throws an empty cup their way.

The twin seated in front of Sonja drags her close, tilting his mask up just high enough to reveal his mouth. He plants his lips against Sonja's in a hungry way that has my hips rocking against Hess without permission. His hand travels to my waist and tightens.

"Hello, Sonja? You're supposed to do the next round?" Georgia huffs in annoyance.

The twin without his tongue down Sonja's throat answers for her. "Abbot's girls." He points to two women in matching cat costumes. They're sitting on either side of a tall, thin man. He wears a slender brown and green wooden mask housing two monstrous faces in one.

"We have names," the blonde cat says, not hiding her irritation. "I'm Dawn, she's Tracy." She points to the second cat, a petite woman with a blue and black pixie cut.

"Dawn and Tracy, truth or dare? And don't say truth. That shit is boring."

"Dare," they answer in unison.

"I dare you two to make out." His voice rises in pitch, signaling his excitement.

"Why are all the dares so sexual?" Tracy complains.

"Is that a no?" the twin presses.

"I didn't say that," Tracy fires back. She leans across Abbot's lap, her hand wrapping around the back of Dawn's neck. Dawn is giggling nervously as Tracy takes her lips.

They kiss several times, their movements growing deeper as they melt into each other, losing themselves to the pleasure.

"Hell yeah. That is hot," Luda cheers from across the fire.

At the sound of his voice, the girls pull apart. Dawn's face is beet red as she presses a hand to her lips and stifles another embarrassed laugh. Tracy looks less than fazed.

"Alright, Alanna—" Tracy starts.

"Why are the girls getting all the action?" Luda bellyaches.

Tracy shakes her head. "Fine, Luda. Truth or dare?"

"Dare, duh," he answers quickly.

"Well, you want to be the center of attention so badly. Why don't you give us all a strip tease?" The rest of the girls cheer, clearly approving of the dare.

Luda doesn't hesitate. "Did Evie put you up to this?" He turns to me. "Evie, If you wanted to see me naked, all you had to do was ask."

My mouth hinges open. "I did not—" But the words dry up as Luda pulls his shirt over his head, rolling his body as the fabric clears his mask and drops to the ground. The sight of his well-muscled torso has me biting my lip. *Damn.* He pops the top of his jeans with a dramatic flourish, sliding them down and kicking off his boots in the same movement. My eyes greedily appraise him. He's glowing beneath the moonlight, his body bare aside from his briefs and mask. Is he waiting to remove the mask last for dramatic effect? I can't tell what I'm more eager to see, what's beneath his mask or beneath his boxers.

Luda runs his fingers beneath the waistband, toying with the fabric. He inches them lower, revealing soft blond curls. I lean forward in my perch on Hess's lap.

"That's enough." Abbot rises, grabbing Luda's clothes and shoving them into his arms. Luda chuckles while he redresses.

"Don't be such a stick in the mud. I know you're intimidated by my equipment, but don't be so hard on yourself. Small cocks need love too. I'm sure Tracy and Dawn—"

Abbot storms toward him, but Ethan jumps between the two.

"He's fucking with you, Abbot. Calm down." He guides the taller man back to his seat.

I'm grinning widely, watching the interaction with amusement. My smile drops as Luda's mask lands in my direction. "Evie"—he takes two predatory steps toward me—"truth or dare?"

"Dare," I answer without hesitation. Hess tenses behind me.

Luda releases a dark laugh that has goosebumps rising on my arms. "I dare you to run and hide somewhere in the ruins. We'll see if you can stay out of sight for ten whole minutes. If you do, we'll let you choose any prize you desire. But if the three of us find you first"—he leans forward, brushing the backs of his knuckles across my cheek before taking my chin between his thumb and forefinger—"you're *ours* for Halloween."

"What do you say, Evie?" Vibrations rumble through my back as Hess whispers behind me.

My words come out breathy and rushed. "Deal. When do the ten minutes start?"

"They started the second you agreed to the dare." Luda's lighthearted energy has shifted into something much darker.

"Tick tock," Reiner says, miming a tap against the top of his wrist. I'm so surprised by the sound of his rich, sultry voice that I simply stare for a moment.

"Run, little monster," Hess growls low in my ear.

"You have a two-minute head start. Then the real monsters are headed your way," Luda adds, his voice taking on a menacing tone.

Hess is still holding me tightly. I unwrap his arm and spring from his lap, darting in the direction of the ruins at the top of the hill. The rest of the group whoops as I take off in a dead sprint. The decision to wear combat boots, even though they don't go with my costume, is really paying off right now.

"You better run, honey!" I recognize Georgia's Southern lilt.

A grin splits my face as adrenaline surges through my veins. My boys may be big and bad, but I've been an athlete my entire life. I'm confident I can win this dare. A wicked, unfed part of me is craving the chance to lose at their hands. I'm wild with the need to know what it would mean to be *theirs* for Halloween. Their girl? Their plaything? What will they do with me if they catch me?

I'm forced to slow down to navigate the tangle of tree roots. Years of water erosion have carved away the ground around the base of the trees, leaving the thick, healthy tendrils raised high above the earth. I race higher and higher, passing a waterfall with a small sparkling pool to my right. A plethora of tiny orange mushrooms grow at the base of every tree and on the edges of the water. The soil becomes less damp as I make my way into higher terrain. Moonlight shines down all around me, revealing the magical sight of shimmering mica flecks in the boulders and gravel scattered across the ground.

There's something special in the air here. It's as if I've stepped into another world. One where fairies exist, and ancient magic lies dormant beneath my feet. My quads flex as I push up over three large drop-offs, finally scrambling to the flattened area that houses the ruins.

A fluttering cloud of startled moths abandon their ruined perches as I plunge through one of the tall openings in the side of a stony wall that's managed to remain standing all these years. The inside of the ruins is teeming with plant life and even more moths. Felled trees and worn rocks litter a budding sapling forest within stone walls long forgotten. Tiny white flowers blanket any bare spaces that have not yet been reclaimed by the forest floor. I suck in a deep breath, my thoughts growing hazy as the honey scent of the last of fall's sweet alyssum surrounds me. Nothing feels real here, and yet it all feels heightened at the same time. It doesn't make sense.

Heavy footsteps pound a path toward my refuge. I whirl, searching the space for a hiding spot. I've taken too long admiring my surroundings. A clutch of collapsed stones near the center of the open room draws my eyes. There's a small gap beneath, no doubt home to more creepy crawlies than I care to imagine. But I bet I can fit inside and I'm fairly certain the guys won't think to check there. Because who in their right mind would crawl into a dark, claustro-phobic cave with God-knows-what inside? *Someone who wants to win.*

I take a single step in that direction and scream as strong arms wrap around my waist, lifting me off the ground and spinning me in a circle. "Caught you, little monster." The spicy cinnamon scent of Hess drenches me in warmth. My feet hit the ground and I shove away from him. I stumble, my balance temporarily unstable after being spun around.

I crash into another firm chest and Luda chuckles above me. "Watch your step, baby."

My feet are clumsy as I jerk away and take several quick steps. My back slams into a warm, hard slab and electricity dances across my skin. I jump away, turning to find Reiner behind me. My gaze flicks in a circle as all three of them close in on me.

"How the fuck did you make it up here so fast?"

"Don't be too hard on yourself, Evie." Luda's hand reaches out to brush along my arm. "This game was rigged from the start. There's no place on Earth you can hide that we won't find you."

"Looks like your ours, tonight," Hess breathes out, his voice husky and rough.

The three of them press in on me, swallowing my small stature beneath their unmatched heights. The air around me is hot and cold at the same time, and buzzing with an energy that has me dizzy and panting.

"Take off your masks," I implore, my body spinning in circles, trying and failing to keep each of the three in my sights at all time.

"The rules were, you only got to choose a prize if you won," Luda reminds me.

"Please," I beg. All three stop their advance. Glances are exchanged in silence. "I need to see you. Please."

"It's almost time anyways, how much harm can it do?" Luda adds with a shrug of his massive shoulders.

"It's not part of the plan," Hess says in a low voice.

"Did you keep your mask on for Evie?" Luda asks Hess.

"It was off very briefly, and I have better control than the rest of you," Hess grumbles.

What the hell are they talking about?

"I'll keep my other mask in place, I promise." Luda sounds giddy. "What about you, Reiner?"

"I... I think I can keep it together." Reiner's voice is throaty and tight.

"You better not slip," Hess says sharply.

"We won't. We practiced. It will all be good," Luda assures him.

Hess shakes his head. "Alright then, maybe Luda's right. It's getting late. And our little monster should get what she wants. But wooden masks only." Hess casts his gaze at the other two as he slides his mask off. My eyes feast on his rugged jaw and masculine features. Sexy would be too dull of a word to describe his roguish good looks. The light in his amber eyes is glowing even more brightly than before. There's something highly unnatural about it. I'm drawn in like a moth succumbing to the fire that will consume it.

"Hell yeah," Luda pumps his fist in the air, slipping his mask off and dropping it to the ground. Luda's face is angular and carved, but slightly feminine in comparison to Hess. His curly, white-blond hair is nearly as pale and lovely as the moonlight shining down around us. His big, bright eyes are greener than should be humanly possible and his lips are soft and full. He has an ethereal beauty that's difficult to put words to. "Come on, Reiner. She wants to see you."

The last of their trio stands, still shrouded by his mask. Reiner's fingers twitch before slowly lifting his black mask. My breath catches at the sight of his dark features. Eyes as veiled as the night sky glimmer beneath the long thick lashes that surround them. He has sharp, masculine features, and a jaw that could have been cut from the very stone of these ruins. He's devastatingly handsome with an exotic loveliness I've never encountered. My gaze lingers on him as he runs a hand through his long, raven locks.

"It's rude to stare, little monster," Hess purrs in my ear. His warm hands slide around my waist, pulling me back against his body. Heat blooms beneath his palms.

"I'm glad you requested no masks." Luda steps in front of me, peering down with a wicked glint in his emerald eyes. "If you hadn't, I wouldn't have been able to do this."

His lips are soft and cool as they press to mine. I sigh against his mouth, breathing in his salty-sea scent. My arms wind around his neck, dragging him nearer. He steps into me, closing the distance so that my body is pressed between him and Hess. His hands cup my cheeks as his lips explore mine. The kisses are soft at first, but as his grip on me tightens, they become more possessive. I moan into him as his tongue presses between my lips, deepening our kiss. Hess dips behind me, his mouth finding my neck and branding it with a heat that lingers long after he's moved past.

Arousal spirals through my middle as his hands slide up my thighs, raising my dress and exposing my skin to the cool night air. Luda continues to claim my mouth with deep, breath-stealing kisses while Hess trails his fingertips across the top of my now-damp panties.

Luda breaks his kiss long enough to grin down at me. "You lost the dare, baby. That means you're ours for Halloween." He turns me so I'm facing Hess and shoves me into his arms. Hess's lips take rough possession of mine. His mouth is so hot it burns and his tongue snakes between my lips like liquid fire. I moan again, my body beginning to writhe between them. Their mouths are heavenly, but I need more. The dampness between my thighs is craving their touch. "And I think I'd like to see that pretty little mouth of yours wrapped around Hess's cock."

Hess grinds against me, his erection digging into my stomach. "Oh my god," I pant, feeling the full size of what awaits me.

"Why don't you get down on your knees and show me just how deep you can take him." Luda's fingers are caressing my breasts as he speaks.

"Why don't you?" I argue back, my nerves getting the better of me.

"Why don't I get down on my knees and suck his cock?" Luda twists me toward him with an eyebrow raised. I bite my lip, unsure what to say. Luda's gaze flicks to Hess and then back to me. "Would you like that?"

My insides turn warm and liquidy as he snares me in that glittering green gaze. "I think so." Truthfully, I don't know. I've never been with more than one man before so this opportunity has never presented itself. "Would you... Is that something you would do?"

"For you, little monster? I'd do just about anything." He slides me toward Reiner. "Keep her company, will you?"

Reiner takes a step closer but leaves a small space between us.

Hess is standing still and statuesque as Luda moves close to him. My mouth goes dry as Luda lowers himself to his knees. His pale hands work like twin ghosts as he unzips Hess's jeans.

"Reiner is more particular about these things. But Hess, well, he and I have known each other in this way for many, many years." Luda's grin is damn near feral.

Hess's hand snaps out, gripping Luda's chin. "You heard our girl. Now less talking, more sucking."

A groan of desire slides from my lips before I can stop it. Hess gives me a smile that's as devilish as they come. My eyes fixate on Luda's hand as he pulls Hess's impressively large cock free from his boxers. Luda wraps his lips around the engorged tip, making me gasp.

Hess drops his hand to Luda's hair, digging his fingers into the curls. He tugs gently, and Luda's mouth glides down the thick shaft, stopping just before the base. My thighs clench as I watch the action. It feels filthy, staring at them during this intimate and forbidden moment. Maybe the filthiest thing I've ever done. Luda drags his full lips back and Hess drops his head, eyes falling shut, as a moan of pure pleasure fills the quiet air around us.

Needy, simpering sounds leave my lips as I watch the two. Luda swallows Hess's length again and again. My fingers bunch in my skirts, raising them higher, to do what? Something, anything. The need for stimulation, for something to ease the tension tightening within me, is overwhelming.

"Touch her, Reiner," Hess growls out. "Can't you see how badly she needs to be touched?"

He's right. I think I may fall dead on the spot if I don't feel the barest whispers of skin against mine. Reiner is silent as he steps up behind me. His hand covers mine, raising it higher and dragging my skirt up with it. A crisp, unidentifiable scent wraps around me. My skin tingles everywhere his fingers connect with it. Once the fabric has cleared my waist, Reiner guides us several feet away. We end up behind a small, half wall with a worn and weathered top. My eyes stay glued to Luda and Hess, even as Reiner slowly bends me over the wall. I reach out automatically, gripping the firm edge. Luda's bobbing rhythm is mesmerizing. Arousal continues to collect as the aching throb between my thighs grows into something all-consuming.

I barely notice as my underwear is dragged down and discarded. Energy buzzes across my inner thighs as Reiner gently pries them open, widening my stance. The first electric touch of his fingers against my bare pussy makes me groan with gratitude. Luda pops Hess's shaft out of his mouth and shifts toward us. He and Hess are both grinning.

"You're even filthier than we dreamed you would be. Look at you, getting off on me choking down Hess's cock." The green in his eyes ignites.

"She's fucking perfect," Hess says, his amber eyes piercing and voice gravelly.

"She sure as hell is," Luda agrees before pressing Hess back into his open mouth.

Reiner slides two fingers inside me and my back arches in pleasure. I'm so worked up from the chase and watching the others that I could come with barely a thought. He pumps into me with a rough, quick pace that has my legs shaking in a matter of seconds. I squirm beneath him and he presses my stomach down harder against the wall I'm currently bent over. His fingers slide up and down my walls, sending pleasure tingling through me. But the longer I watch the others, the emptier I feel. My eyes are trained on the size of Hess's cock. Fingers are nothing compared to *that*.

"Reiner," I breathe. "I need more. Please." Reiner stiffens behind me, his movements slowing.

Luda pulls free from Hess with a laugh. "I think she's jealous that I've got a cock and she doesn't."

"Is that what it is, Evie? Do you want him to fill your cunt the way I'm filling Luda's throat to the brim?" Hess growls the words out.

"Yes." I gasp, not caring how desperate and needy I sound in the moment.

"More, Reiner. You won't break her. Give her what she needs," Hess commands.

They both stay focused on us as Reiner takes up position behind me. The head of his cock nudges at my entrance and my eyes go wide. *Holy huge—* He spreads my pussy, pressing the first few inches inside and I can't help but cry out. He's thick, so unexpectedly thick. Well, what the hell was I expecting? The man is fucking huge. He was bound to be well proportioned elsewhere.

My grip on the stone wall tightens as he presses in deeper. My pelvis smacks against the stone as his first thrust leaves me breathless and starry-eyed.

"Holy shit," Luda groans. "That is the hottest thing—" His words die off as Hess jerks his head back, stuffing his cock back inside his mouth before he can say anything else. Hess starts to move his hips, using the hand in Luda's hair to control the movement. Behind me, Reiner picks up his pace too. The buzzing sensation from Reiner's girthy length extends deep into my core. His body is practically vibrating as he ruts into me with swift, hard thrusts.

"Oh, yes..." I mumble, as Reiner sets a pace and intensity that has me chasing a powerful orgasm. I take a moment to think about the situation I currently find myself in. A night that had every possibility of being shitty and, at one point, deadly, has turned into one of the hottest and most unexpected experiences of my life. I peer over my shoulder and my body tenses. Reiner's features are twisted, dark. *Why does he look like that?* He grips my face, pivoting it toward Luda and Hess.

My attention moves away from the tricks my eyes play upon me, to the other two men. Hess moves a second hand to Luda's hair and fucks his face harder than before. Behind me, Reiner thrusts into me more forcefully. It takes me a minute to realize they're taking cues from each other.

"Harder, Reiner," I say breathlessly, testing my theory. Reiner obliges, slamming into me hard enough to make me yelp. Across from us, Hess moves faster, his cock disappearing fully into Luda's mouth with each stroke.

The new pressure and angle have a steady stream of mewling and moans pouring out of me. Reiner is grunting behind me, the sounds growing louder with each passing second. My climax is close. Every part of me is tightening, preparing for the ultimate release. The sight of Luda gagging as Hess hits the back of his throat shatters the last of my control. The climax is so powerful it steals my vision. I scream as what feels like the continuous jolts of electricity emptying into my core prolong my orgasm and make me fight for breath.

Hess gasps across from me, his body stiffening as he slams home one last time before emptying down Luda's throat with a whimper of relief. Reiner's hands tighten to a bruising hold as his thrusts become jerky and clipped. He roars his climax to the fog that's descended upon us sometime in the last few minutes. I jump as a jolt of electricity more powerful than the others zaps at my clit. I come again, moaning and simpering as Reiner's warm, thick cum fills me up.

Chapter 2

Hess

The high from my climax mixed with the overly sweet scent in the air has me lightheaded. Evie is still moaning, her body draped over the wall as Reiner fucks into her hard enough to make the sounds of his pelvis slapping against her ass echo around the ruins.

"Our girl is a freak," Luda whispers, smirking up at me as he wipes his mouth clean. I offer him my hand and drag him to my lips. He sighs into my mouth. I wasn't sure how Evie would feel about the relationships between the three of us. But her eagerness to watch us together has put some of my fears at ease.

When I pull back, Luda's emerald eyes are simmering with the demon within. I prefer to have him in his other form, but the human skin he's chosen has me questioning if we should slip into these bodies more often.

Our gazes shift back to Evie. Reiner finishes inside her. Evie's beautiful face contorts with pleasure as she comes around his dick once more. A twinge of jealousy awakens in my gut. I was hoping to claim her first, but Reiner needed this. The poor guy was terrified to touch her. She is human, after all. I suppose I'll just have to be the first to claim her in our other forms.

Luda moves toward Evie and I catch him by the arm. "We don't have much time."

"Relax. The hardest part is over. You got her here. Everything else will fall into place."

I snarl. "Getting her here didn't exactly go as planned."

"We'll tie up loose ends later."

He tries to step away again, and I clutch his shoulder. "But if the ceremony—"

"Come on, Hess. I want her in this body. We still have time. The others had their night. This one is ours," Luda grouses, palming the prominent ridge in his jeans.

I sigh, giving in. Luda always seems to get his way. Meanwhile I'm stuck being the responsible one. I can't complain too much. It's the reason I was chosen as the one to retrieve Evie. I wouldn't trade that experience for the world.

"Fine. As long as you're finished before the ritual begins, I don't care what you do."

He grips me by the arm, dragging us both to where Evie lies limp and panting over the crumbling ruins. "You mean what *we* do. Just try to have some fun. This is the best night of our lives. Hers too. She just doesn't know it yet."

Luda crouches in front of Evie. She lifts her head, her eyes glazed. Her body twitches occasionally as remnants of Reiner's power flicker through her. It probably wasn't the best idea to let him go first. Of the three of us, he has the least control of his powers in this form. If Evie's screams of pleasure were any indication, though, she didn't mind the stray bolts here and there.

"Hey, little monster. Can you take more?" Luda's voice takes on a hypnotic tone and I know in that moment he's edging on the line of coercion. Which means despite his casual demeanor, he's nervous. Evie needs to accept us. *All three of us.* But I knew from the moment I saw her that she was the one. The others will realize in due time that she was made for us. This is just the first night of many.

Evie pulls her lip between her teeth, nodding. Reiner lifts her up, bringing her to stand and supporting her weight as she regains her footing. Luda pulls his shirt over his head and drapes it on the stone wall. Evie's eyes devour the sight of Luda's muscled form. Our girl's got a type. Luckily the three of us all fit the mold. Luda hops up onto the wall and faces me.

"Bring her here." He pats his lap. Reiner scoops her up, moving around the wall and depositing her so that she's straddling Luda. "Let's take this off for a bit." He glides her dress over her head, leaving her in nothing but a lacy gold bra. With the dress out of the way, I have a clear view of Evie's body. My tongue dips out, wetting my lips as Luda lines her up. Reiner's release is already dripping down her thighs, spinning my mind with fantasies of all three of us, filling her with our cum until it's pouring out of every one of her holes.

Evie exhales a sound of pleasure as Luda guides her down the length of his shaft. Her legs are already shaky, but from the way Luda has his hands wrapped around her waist, I don't think he's expecting her to do any of the work. My eyes are held to the spot where their bodies connect. Luda's cock disappears inside her, making her whimper as she hits his pelvis. When he glides her up again, his cock is wet and shiny with her arousal. A possessive growl sneaks free from my carefully guarded façade. Luda's bottle-green eyes snap my way.

"Why don't we turn you around so Hess can find out how good you taste?" he murmurs in her ear. Evie nods, gasping when Luda spins her around to face me. He bounces her again and again as I approach, making her take every inch of him. I stalk toward them, the predator within me rising to the surface. Evie's blue eyes track my movements as I descend before her. Luda pumps into her once more and then stills, keeping her seated with his full length inside.

I slide my hands beneath her knees, pressing them up, and opening her fully to me. She gasps, no doubt feeling every-thing more intensely with Luda filling her up. My tongue dips out, brushing along her clit and I'm instantly wishing I could take my true form. *The things I'm going to do to her when I can use my real tongue...*

Evie sucks in a sharp breath, making me grin against her wet flesh. I gorge myself on her pussy, not sparing a second for the buildup. We don't have much time left. She jumps, trying to move, writhe, squirm, do something. But she's trapped. Impaled on Luda's cock with no way to escape the ravenous feasting of my overeager mouth. Her body is pliant, responsive, and oh so easy to please. Her moans grow louder and Luda reacts to her heightened arousal. He slips his palms beneath her ass, gently rocking her with his cock inside, while I continue laving and lapping at her clit.

She cries out as she comes and Luda groans with her. I have no doubt he can feel the keen tightening of her perfect cunt around his hardened length. It looks like heaven. But I wouldn't switch our positions. Ravishing pussy is my specialty, and I want Evie to feel exactly what she's getting herself into. I release her clit, dropping low to rim the spot just where Luda has her skin stretched wide. My tongue glides across the tender space where their bodies meet. They both groan from the sensation. My need to feed is still unsatiated, but I rise to my feet.

This next part needs to be quick. The others will be summoning us soon.

Luda starts bouncing her up and down again. I can't stop the grin that's stretching across my face. Making our girl come is going to be my new favorite addiction. I can't deny how good Evie looks, sitting astride Luda's cock, taking his length like a fucking champ. She looked just as good getting railed by Reiner. I'm very familiar with his dick. His girth would be a struggle for any woman. But of the three of us, I'm the largest. Especially in my true form. And I'm looking forward to filling Evie so full she can't tell if she's swept up in the sweetest dream or trapped within her darkest nightmare. I suppose as *our* girl, she'll always be skirting the line between the two.

Luda's features are pinched in concentration. He's close. I grip Evie's face, sinking my tongue in her mouth and showing her how filthy and sweet she tastes. I pull back, squeezing her jaw a little tighter. "Be a good little monster and come for us. *Now.*"

Luda reaches around to toy with her freshly devoured clit and Evie explodes. Her voiceless cry comes out as a puff of hot breath that dissipates into the swirling white mist that's shrouding us from the world outside. Luda follows her into the void, groaning as he pumps her full of his release. "Good girl."

Reiner emerges from his shadowy perch, his eyes hungry and bright. He's always enjoyed watching. "It's almost time."

I lift Evie off Luda, setting her on the ground and holding tightly to her as she finds her footing. She looks sexy as hell clad in nothing but a gold bra and white combat boots. My eyes drop between her thighs to where the mixture of Reiner and Luda's spend is dripping down her quivering legs. I swipe a finger through the glistening, white liquid and raise it to Evie's mouth. Her eyes widen in surprise as I push the coated finger between her lips.

"Suck it clean," Luda coos in her ear, moving up behind her. She obeys, her lips wrapping tight and sucking on my finger until all evidence of their cum has disappeared down her throat. Damn our girl really is perfect. "Filthy, filthy, filthy." Grinning, Luda spins her around and presses a kiss to her swollen lips.

We help her into her dress, not bothering to give her back her panties. She won't be needing those anymore. The three of us slide our wooden masks back into place, exchanging hidden looks and nodding. Our human masks may have slipped a few times, but overall, I'm impressed. My true form is fighting for freedom. I'm certain the others are in a similar boat. An immense amount of magic went into the masks. The ornate decorations tie us to our temporary human forms. For most, simply slipping it off would result in a full-blown transformation. Few have the control needed to lose the mask and stay "human". The fact that none of us shifted fully out of our current skin while performing sexual acts for Evie is a goddamn miracle.

I sweep her up into my arms, loving the way her scent has been mixed with all of ours. She smells perfect like this. "It's time for the main event," I tell her, smirking beneath my mask as we leave the ruins behind and make our way toward the bonfire.

"That didn't count as a main event?" she says, her voice slightly hoarse from all the moaning and crying out. I decide in that moment to make it my personal goal to ensure her voice never has a chance to fully recover again. I'll have her mute if I must, so long as the loss of her voice comes from the screams of her passion at our hands.

"Not even close, little monster," I breathe into her ear. Evie shivers.

"There they are!" Ethan claps as we approach. He's joined by several others. Evie buries her face in my shoulder.

"Please put me down before I die of embarrassment," she murmurs against my shirt.

"Being fucked until you can't walk straight is nothing to be embarrassed about," I tease. It earns me a slap on the arm.

"Hess," she warns.

"Fine, you can walk." I set her down but keep her hand in mine.

The rest of the group is gathered around the fire. The girls laugh and drink, chatting with one another. But the men are restless. Tension fills the air, thicker than the fog that continues to close in around us. The witching hour is nearly upon us. I nod to the twins. Rhylan rises and strides quickly into the darkened tree line.

"I know that look! But all three? Honey, you are an over-achiever!" Kodi's shadow match calls out, giggling and pointing our way. The front of her silver body suit is unzipped farther every time I look over at her. Is that Kodi's doing? If he's not careful, she'll end up tits out before the ritual has even started. She's still laughing when Kodi grasps her by the back of the neck and bends her over his lap, swatting her ass and making her cry out.

"Behave, Georgia." His demeanor is cool, calm, and collected, betraying nothing of the beast within. I've known Kodi for centuries. It's a miracle he's managed to keep it together as long as he has. Georgia is a handful. She'll be in for it when Kodi takes his true form. The thought makes me chuckle.

"What's so funny?" Evie quirks an eyebrow up at me. Her cheeks are still ruddy from Georgia's comment.

"You'll see." I smile, not bothering to explain. She lets out a frustrated huff. *Not long now.*

The four of us settle into our spot at the edge of the fire, Evie nestled between Luda and me, with Reiner on Luda's other side. My hand falls to Evie's thigh out of instinct. Luda's hand lands on the other and we exchange a look. His mask hides his emotions but I'm certain he's feeling the same buzzing excitement and possessiveness that I am. I wasn't certain of the choice when the Shadowed One assigned all three of us to the same mortal. Most of the others were assigned as singles. One of us, and one girl. Abbot even got two mortals. Then again, his true form likely needs more than one. My initial reaction was shock and jealousy, even though Reiner and Luda are my closest friends. I understand we're the only species besides the twins that has more than one prince left, but still. It was difficult to trust in their dark guidance and knowing.

The last few hours have changed everything. Now that I've met Evie, I'm certain the Shadowed One knew exactly what they were doing. The dynamic in our group feels indescribably right.

Rhylan strides through the mist, carrying a wooden slab with eleven golden goblets. My pulse picks up, thundering a tune of divine expectation that has my entire body humming. The group quiets, and all eyes land on the brilliant, golden vessels. They shine in the firelight, their glossy surfaces reflecting the flickering flames. Several men look to me. The masks prevent me from deciphering anyone's expressions, but I don't need to see their faces to know what they're thinking. We've waited so long for this moment.

It's time to begin.

Nerves I'm unaccustomed to spark through me as I rise to address those present. Fear sends a myriad of alternate endings to our current situation flooding through my mind. I shove them away, breathing deeply. This will work out. It was prophesized. There is no other way.

"My brothers"—I circle my hidden gaze around the bonfire —"we have waited lifetimes for this opportunity. Sixteen years ago, a devastating plague spread throughout our realm. We all lost more than can be comprehended. Our families, our loved ones, our people." My chest tightens. Those were dark days. "We pleaded with the Shadowed

One for a chance to save the dwindling species of our realm. In their great wisdom, the Shadowed One chose, for each of us, a human bride. She was to be the one who helped to ensure the lineage of each house and species would not be lost forever. It has taken all these years to bring each of our shadow matches into the fold, but with the retrieval of Evie this evening, we've successfully secured all eleven brides."

The men rally with cheers of triumph and relief. My heart swells with their excitement, but the feeling fades as I take in the confused faces of the brides. Evie looks up at me, her discomfort evident. Rhylan passes the golden cups around, ensuring one male from each group takes a goblet into their possession. The contents of the cup are earthy and floral, brewed with herbs specific to our realm. Each of us removes the small, sharp thimble that we've kept housed in our pockets these last sixteen years. I drag the tip across the pad of my thumb, watching as a drop of sizzling crimson wells up on the surface. When a thick drop of satisfactory size has formed, I tap my finger on the goblet, allowing my blood to disappear into the dark liquid. Luda and Reiner add their blood to the cup. The droplets dip beneath the surface as the liquid begins to glow. The others follow our lead.

"Okay, whatever this is, it's kinky." Sonja giggles.

"Yeah, what is going on? Because it's starting to feel very cult-y," Cami adds with a raised brow.

"Oh come on, girls, it's just a bit of spooky Halloween fun," Georgia says, grinning widely.

Evie sits quietly. Her thoughts churn with uncertainty, and my anxiety surges. "The contents within each of these goblets contain just a drop of our blood. By consuming it, you'll be granted a temporary taste of the life and pleasure that can be yours, if you choose it." I drop my gaze to Evie, who is now staring at the cup. "And while it was never our intention to deceive you, we must admit, those of us before you are not of the human realm. Beneath our disguises hide a variety of monstrous creatures. Upon drinking from your cups, our true forms will be revealed."

"Ooooh, scary," Georgia whispers to Cami.

"I do not wish for any of you to misunderstand. *We are monsters.* Nightmarish beings from tales told around camp-fires in the dark. But on my life, I assure you, we will not harm you. You are precious to us in a way you will never understand. If you drink, do so willingly, and with the knowledge that monsters are very real." The cups are handed to each of the brides as they continue to look around in confusion.

"Wait, you want us to drink your blood?" Cami asks, releasing a nervous laugh.

"Yes," Ethan answers, running his fingers along the length of her scarlet hair.

Evie peers down into the cup, then flicks her gaze between the three of us. "You guys are serious?" she asks, wrapping her fingers around the wide top of the goblet.

I nod. "Don't be afraid."

She sucks in a deep breath, her bright blue eyes sparkling with curiosity. "I'm not." And just like that, she raises the cup to her lips, taking a deep pull of the enchanted liquid.

"Hell yeah, Evie! Let's do this." Georgia drains her own cup.

"Honestly this wouldn't be the weirdest thing I've done for a guy." Cami laughs before taking a drink.

"I mean, it is Halloween." Dawn interlocks her arm with Tracy as they both down their drinks.

The posture of each masked man relaxes as, one by one, the shadow matches finish off their glasses. I turn to Evie, acutely aware of the shift in her energy. Her pupils dilate, blocking out the brilliant blue of her eyes, and her mouth opens in a gasp. A demon's blood is a powerful amplifier of all sensations, particularly lust. It is especially potent to those who consume it willingly. Evie throws her head back, a low moan spilling forward.

It's working.

I rip my mask off, tossing it to the ground. The rest of the men follow suit, each of us itching to free our *other* selves.

"It's time," I announce, gently taking Evie's chin between my fingers. "Trust us and know...there's no need to scream."

Chapter 3
Evie

A starry warmth spreads through my chest. The world around me takes on a soft, golden glow. Liquid lightning courses through my veins, crackling up my spine and bleeding into my very soul. A flush of burning need swims through my core, sending a flood of arousal between my thighs. My skin is too tight, my breathing too fast. I'm hot, cold, tingling, and *so fucking horny*. My thighs clench and I rub them together, desperate for the friction to ease some of the pent-up need that's over-taking me. I moan, unable to stay quiet any longer.

"It's time," Hess announces to the group. Time for what? What in the hell was in that drink? The men drop their masks, and I get my first look at the faces of the others. Hess takes my cheeks in his hand, his amber eyes glowing with a fire that is impossible to look away from. "Trust us and know...there's no need to scream."

The world slows down as the men around me all rise to their full heights and begin to strip. My eyes drag along the bodies of all three of the men now surrounding me. "Why would I scream—" I begin to ask, but a sharp howling tears my gaze away from them.

Georgia is lying back, her body writhing as some sort of beast leers over her. What the fuck is that? It's massive, over eight feet tall, with thick black fur covering it from head to toe. A long muzzle with impressively large fangs dips a tongue out, running it up Georgia's neck. She moans, reaching down to unzip her jumpsuit fully. "Is that..." I start, but what can I say? In Kodi's place, there now stands what can only be described as a literal fucking werewolf. But this one isn't like the movies. It has six arms, shining silver eyes, and a line of sharp metallic ridges that runs down its back from nape to tail.

Terror clambers up through my lust. What if it eats Georgia? What if it kills her? The beast removes the rest of her clothes until she's naked beneath him. I open my mouth to say something, to warn her, but then Kodi drops his muzzle between her thighs and starts to lick. Okay, so he's not exactly eating her. I mean not in the way I was expecting. My desire surges as I watch the two. All of this has taken place in a matter of a few fractured seconds that sit bubbling in my sexually charged thoughts.

"Eyes up here, baby. You don't want to miss the show," Luda says, tipping my chin toward him. My confusion grows as I watch ten long, sharp claws emerge from the ends of Luda's fingers. He turns to Hess, running his nails down the other man's spine. Blood spills out and Hess screams. I jump to my feet. My movements halt as I notice something wriggling beneath Hess's split skin. Something that looks very much alive.

My mouth drops open as two massive, blood-red wings burst from the gaping wound in Hess's back. A second later his screams turn to songs of pleasure. He tugs at the corner of the split skin on his shoulder, peeling it away. My heart races as Hess removes every bit of golden-tan skin, revealing a rough, red surface beneath. He throws his head back, crying to the sky as two thick, copper-colored horns spiral up out of his skull. They jut into the air, growing over a foot in length.

My gaze slides over his new body. His deep, red skin is covered with the cracked markings of sunbaked earth. Soft orange light spills out from every fissure and fault, giving the illusion that fire is burning beneath his flesh. I want to admire him more, but the sounds of ripping skin snap my eyes back to Luda.

Luda's body twists and bends. He stretches his pale skin wider and wider, working it loose until it's completely translucent, then he slides out of it like a snake. The body that emerges is breathtakingly vibrant. Shiny green scales cover Luda's new form. They shift, changing from a pale seafoam to a deep emerald depending on how he moves. He reaches his hands over his head, stretching and length-ening his body. My heart tightens when he cries out. Six gashes split open between his ribs. Another two open above his hip bones. Dark webbed protrusions push outward from the slits in his skin. *Are those fins?*

He's emerged as some sort of sea creature. More webbing grows between his clawed fingers, which change in color to a green so dark it's nearly black. A ring of sharp, thin horns encircle the top of his shimmery head, giving the illusion he's wearing a crown of ghostly turret shells.

An inhuman scream comes from my left, where Reiner is currently mid-transformation. He's using his own sharp claws to shred his dark skin. Raking his finger down from his human face all the way to his feet. The discarded outer layers drop to the ground in bloody, twisted ribbons. The body that's revealed beneath his bronzed skin is nothing like the others.

Reiner's form is sleek, black, and shiny enough for me to see my reflection in his abdomen. His metallic exoskeleton reflects the light of the fire, giving him the iridescent appearance of an oil spill. Two obsidian horns press through his temples, curving down and forward until they're framing his monstrous face. He twists his body, shaking off the last of his human flesh. That's when I see it, *the tail.*

A dark, braided tail rears up and over him like a scorpion. The tip of it illuminates, producing a thin line of electricity from one end to the other. The electricity races along his tail and shudders across his body, lighting him up as small, arcing bolts of energy dance across his outer shell.

Reiner's blinding, black eyes drop to me, and I take my first breath in ages. My neck aches from craning it up to look. They're all well over eight feet now. Hess's wings make him even taller. All three of them are staring down at me. And while they differ in color and shape, they all share the same unique mouth. Their jaws stretch from ear to ear and are filled with hundreds of needlelike pointed teeth. Hess opens his mouth, letting an extra-long, forked tongue dip out, swiping at the air before retreating behind his many teeth.

Holy shit. They really are monsters.

"Evie?" Hess asks, his voice slightly gravellier than in his human form. "You still with us?"

My eyes jump from body to body, taking in everything that makes them unique from one another. They're terrifying, monstrous, the stuff of nightmares. And yet...there's something so beautiful and alluring about each one. My fingers grasp at air by my sides. I *need* to touch them.

I reach out my hand to skim across Hess's abdomen. The deep muscles flex at my touch. His skin is burning. My eyes drop to the massive cock jutting out from between his huge thighs. It's bright red and covered in deep ridges that run all the way around. My pussy clenches as I stare at the way the dark, raised veins pulse along the girthy shaft. I drop my hand down to grip it and groan as it twitches in my palm.

"She's with us, alright." Luda grins.

One of Hess's massive hands covers mine, squeezing my fingers more tightly around his shaft. The other grips the front of my dress. Smoke curls up from his palm as he runs it down the front of the fabric, burning through the thin lace and leaving two charred black pieces behind. Reiner moves in behind me, grasping the ruined dress by the shoulders and sliding it off my body. The closer Reiner gets to me, the more the hairs on my arms rise. My skin tingles and thrills everywhere his charged skin touches mine.

Luda moves to join the other two. His claw-tipped finger flicks out, snipping my bra at its center and straps. The pieces hit the ground, leaving me fully bare to the hungry stares of three beautifully terrifying monsters.

Hess leans close, the heat of him radiating through the small space that separates us. "Let's show everyone who you belong to."

I don't have time to scream before Hess takes my waist and launches off the ground. His massive, bat-like wings beat in long, hard strokes as they carry us up into the sky. Air whooshes past us, sending my hair whipping around my face. We're well out of reach of the others when Hess halts our ascent. We hover in midair. His wings are spread wide as he gently sweeps them up and down, keeping us suspended above the bonfire.

"I don't mind sharing." He drops his head low, running his nose along my throat. His smoky, spicy scent makes my head swim. "But the demon within me is a predator. And if I don't get a few minutes of alone time with you first, then I won't be able to trust myself not to destroy anyone else who has the audacity to touch what's *mine*."

My world turns upside down as Hess flips me over and drops me several feet. My cry is cut short when he swoops beneath me, catching me by my thighs. My back slams against his chest and my head swings between his thighs. Hess's dark chuckle rumbles through me. "Are you scared now, little monster?"

I consider his words. I'm hanging upside down, fully naked, several stories above the ground, in the clutches of a literal monster. Despite the unusual circumstances, I grin. The intense emotions rushing through my body stem from excitement, not fear. "No."

"Good. Because there's no turning back now."

I'm facing away from Hess, which means there's no warning before his inhuman tongue plunges deep inside me. I yelp, my body tensing at the unexpected fullness. Hess's tongue is warm as it slides in and out, lapping up my arousal and making my body bow with pleasure. My arms flail, unable to grasp anything but the dark breeze that sweeps across the night sky. "*Relax.*" His grip on my thighs tightens. Hess speaks with his tongue still deep inside.

Wait, he didn't speak it. I just heard it. "*That's right, Evie, I've been in your head this whole time. I know just how filthy you truly are.*"

My mind snaps back to our conversation in the truck. He really was able to read my thoughts. "Asshole," I snap, as embarrassment floods my cheeks.

"I would think being suspended above a crowd and having your pussy eaten by a demon would trump the embarrassment of me knowing you wanted to fuck me as soon as we met."

He's got a point. I'd laugh if I wasn't so busy moaning. My current position gives me the perfect view of those below. Sonja is sandwiched between two identical creatures who I can only assume are the twins. Their bodies are humanoid in shape, but their black and violet markings and the swirling black mist that seems to bleed from their pores gives them away as something far more sinister. Sonja is bent forward, with one twin fucking into her from behind, while the other drives his cock down her throat. The shadows themselves are alive with movement. I gasp as the smoke solidifies into a wispy tendril and plunges into Sonja's ass. The sight of her being spit-roasted and shadow-fucked unlocks a darkness in me that has me craving to be used in a similar way. Lust burrows into my tissues as Hess's tongue tows me closer to an orgasm that I know is going to shatter my very being.

Cami's vibrant red hair catches my attention next. She's sitting astride what I can only describe as a literal fucking dragon. The creature below her has deep blue scales, thick clawed hands, and a long fang-filled jaw that reminds me of a sapphire-colored crocodile. The dragon rocks Cami up and down on a cock that's so impressively large I can see it from here. A long, black tongue stretches past its many fangs, reaching all the way to Cami's clit. It licks at her clit while she rides its massive member. Cami's moans are audible even from up here. The monster roars and shiny, blue liquid comes pouring out from between her thighs. I'm certain the monster just came, but despite the flood of dark cum, he continues drilling up inside her.

The bellow of something hideously large pulls my gaze away from Cami and her monster. Something resembling a mix between a petrified tree and the largest spider I've ever seen has two girls strung up in a mass of green vines. I recognize the pleasure-filled faces of Dawn and Tracy. Their monster has two moss-covered bodies that meet in a tangle of sharp, bent legs. Two faces, two torsos, two long, twisted cocks. Both girls are being taken by the twin torsos while an array of writhing vines stuff every other hole they have. Is that Abbot? Is he both of those creat—

My thoughts are short-circuited as my core contracts around Hess's talented tongue. The slippery appendage continues to work my tightening pussy until every ounce of pleasure has been drawn from my body. He slides it out, flicking the forked end over my clit and making me come again instantly. I don't know if it's the drink, or the blood, or the fact that I'm hanging upside down but the post-orgasmic ecstasy feels more potent than ever before.

"It's the blood. It's an aphrodisiac, and it intensifies every sensation when you're with us." Hess's voice rumbles

through my mind. That makes sense. I just came twice, and my body is already craving more.

Moans, bellows, screeches, and roars all rise from below us. My mind grows dizzy as more and more blood rushes to my head. Hess flips me upright and I gasp as the moon takes its rightful place above me once more.

"We can't have you passing out."

My hands wrap around Hess's neck, grateful to finally have something to hold onto. His erection is hot beneath me. I roll my hips, wanting, no, *needing* him like this. Hess is the only one of the three that I haven't gotten to fuck yet, and I've wanted him since the first moment we met. He groans, bringing his tip to my entrance.

"I wanted you too, baby." Hess is even bigger than I imagined he would be. My muscles tighten, instinctively trying to force him out. But as the heat from his ribbed length sinks into my flesh, my body melts around him. He probes into me with smooth, slow thrusts. Pain radiates through my sensitive flesh from the way he's stretching me, pushing my body to the very edges of how much it can take.

"Do you want the others to have a turn?" Hess thrusts deeper inside me.

"Yes," I answer without hesitation. Being with Hess is hotter than anything I've experienced, but I can't help but wonder what would happen if Luda and Reiner joined us.

"Come for me again, and I'll let them have their way with you."

His words make me shiver despite the smoldering heat that rises from his glowing flesh. Hess grips my ass, lifting my hips and giving himself access to a new angle. My jaw slams open as the ridges of his cock stroke me with a sinful pressure that has my eyes crossing. He pumps into me faster and I reach up, taking his horns to stabilize myself. I still can't believe we're up in the air. He is literally fucking me while flying.

Hess moans as my fingers grip the copper base of his vestigial features. I squeeze them tighter, milking the smooth, metallic horns with my palms. Hess moves faster, growling in my ear and sinking into me with a punishing pace. Pressure builds, growing and growing. The heat of his cock and the ridges on his shaft have me lost to a blinding pleasure that has me certain I'm burning alive. Pain flares within me as my muscle squeeze around his thickness.

How can everything feel so fucking good? Pleasure and heat engulf me, leaving me burning like a falling star in the wake of the explosive climax. He growls his approval, slowing his movements and staring down at me with an unmatched wickedness in his eyes.

"Did you come?" I pant.

"Oh no, little monster. I won't finish inside you until I've had my fill of every part of that sweet, little body." His tongue coasts up my throat and passes along my lips. "And until it's my turn again..."

A scream shatters the air around us as Hess releases me. I plummet toward the ground, barely recognizing the rushing waters of the creek below me. I'm only feet from impact when Luda's shimmering emerald form breeches the surface. Strong arms catch me, and Luda's laughter surrounds us.

"I got you." He draws me close, swimming us to the shallower water.

"Motherfucker," I rasp. My entire body is shaky with adrenaline.

Hess's dark chuckle draws my gaze to where he and Reiner stand near the edge of the bank. "You better watch that mouth, Evie, or I'll have Luda stuff it with his cock. Then you'll have no choice but to keep your insults to yourself." His fang-filled grin makes him all the more dangerous-looking, and dammit if I don't find him even more attractive like this.

"I like that plan," Luda muses. "But I intend to fill you up in a few other ways first."

The water ripples around us, and I'm wholly unprepared for the mass of tangled, green tentacles that burst through the surface. They dance through the air, unfurling and revealing the hundreds of white circular suckers that line the undersides. *Oh my god.*

Chapter 4
Luda

Evie's dilated eyes go wide at the sight of my tentacles. Her shocked expression fills me with satisfaction. We're all demons, but these extra parts of me are something I wouldn't sacrifice for anything. Not Hess's wings or Reiner's tail.

"Are those—" Evie starts, but I have her wrapped up and lifted out of the water before she can finish her sentence.

"Tentacles," I confirm, sliding one inside her without warning. Her body is so much warmer than the cold water we're standing in. An aftereffect of Hess, no doubt. She jumps, her mouth gaping as her body accepts the slippery appendage. My eyes feast on her pussy as I add a second and third tentacle. The smooth tendrils work independently. Which means right now, they're each stroking a different spot inside her.

I raise Evie higher out of the water, slowly rotating her so that everyone can see. I wait until her ass is facing Hess and Reiner, then slide a tentacle inside her tight hole.

"Luda!" she cries out, flailing at the unexpected intrusion. This part of her is unchartered, and I knew the second I got her in the water that I wouldn't be able to resist.

"What's the matter, baby?" I can't help the grin that's plastered across my reptilian face.

"I..." she chokes out, still squirming, "That's—" I can't tell if she's embarrassed or uncomfortable.

"Hess," I holler. "Which is it?"

"Both. Give her a distraction." He chuckles, reading her thoughts. Which *is* a skill I'm envious of.

"Easily done." I raise another tentacle from the water, guiding it up the front of her bare body. I rotate her again so she's facing toward me. I can't wait to see the look on her face.

"Luda—" she starts again. I lay a tentacle across her open folds, latching my sucker to her clit. Evie's eyes roll back in her head. Drool drips from her open mouth. That's exactly the reaction I was hoping for.

"Showoff!" Reiner calls from the shore. I'm sure he's eager for his turn with our perfect bride.

Evie's practically gone catatonic. She's limp, silent, floating in space with my tentacles stuffed inside her. It truly is a beautiful sight. I let the muscles around the circular suckers contract and she jolts back to life. She moans so loudly that some of the couples nearby turn our way. I don't mind the other demons getting an eyeful of my girl. It's the whole reason I have her suspended above the water instead of splashing around in it. She looks damn good like this, and not a single other man here can do what I'm doing.

Evie writhes as I work my tentacles in a complex array of motions that has her screaming. Each tentacle is doing its best to ruin her. Three in her pussy, one in her ass, and a sea of powerful suckers massaging her clit with a merciless rhythm. Evie comes hard enough to squeeze around all four. Arousal squirts from her opening, running along the tentacles and raining down into the water below.

"Holy shit," Reiner breathes from the spot where he and Hess are soaking up every second of Evie's orgasmic bliss. They're both hard. Hess palms his erection. Reinier's fists clench and unclench by his sides as energy crackles across his skin. Even I have to admit the way she just came is the hottest thing I've ever seen.

"If you're not careful, you're going to sucker her damn clit right off," Hess warns.

My tentacles keep at her, forcing out three more orgasms and working every inch of her squirming body until she begs for a break. She gasps in relief as I unlatch the suckers from her overly sensitive nub. I withdraw my tentacles more slowly, loving the guttural groan she makes as I empty her. I may be giving her clit a moment to rest, but I'm a monster with needs, and mercy has never been my strength.

Evie drops into my arms, her lungs working overtime. The edge of the creek is lined with boulders of various sizes. I choose a smooth, flat stone that's large enough to accommodate us both. Evie is still panting as I drape her chest over the rock. Hess and Reiner move closer, watching everything with greedy gazes.

A splash sounds from behind me as Aegrin slams his shadow match, Alanna, up against the bank on the opposite side. His silver body ripples as he switches to his amphibious form. He swipes a grey, split tongue out, lapping at her throat. His face vanishes beneath the surface and doesn't come back up again. He doesn't have tentacles, but he can breathe underwater. It's a trait most of us water demons possess. Alanna starts moaning, her hands grasping at the soft dirt above her head as his mouth takes her beneath the water. I'll have to try that on Evie next time.

Evie's breathing slows. "Rested and recharged?" I tease.

"Hardly." She giggles but makes no move to leave this position.

I slide a single tentacle inside her from behind, swirling the tip to ensure she's still warmed up and ready to take me. She pushes her hips back, and I accept her invitation with a wicked thrust of my hips. My cock glides through her wet folds with ease, disappearing deep into her center. I settle there for a moment. Having her in my human form was so fucking good, but taking her in my demon form is down-right deadly.

The urge to fill her with my cum again has me ready to burst after a few languid shifts of my hips. I consider fighting the urge, but I've had my alone time. Reiner's body is practically blinding me with the storm brewing beneath the surface of his metallic exterior. I'll at least make sure my devious little monster comes with me. My shaft is deco-rated with circular markings that mimic my suckers. By shifting my angle, I'm able to glide the largest of those markings to Evie's G-spot.

She bucks back against me, mewling as I hit the same spot again and again, keeping a steady, firm rhythm that will ensure her cum covers my dick before I flood her pussy. Six rolling thrusts later and Evie tosses her head back, crying out her release and squeezing me until my own release pours out of me.

My tentacles thrash as I empty into her. The high from Evie's cunt is unlike anything I could have imagined. She's a drug, and I'm a slave to my addiction for her already. I drag Evie into the water, cooling her sensi-tive passage and readying her to take more. Preparing her for Reiner is the least I can do after taking my sweet time with her. Her head falls to my shoulder. She simpers as I splash cold water over her sore pussy. She's taken a lot, but we're nowhere near done with her.

"I think she needs another dose if she's going to make it through this," I call up to Hess. He nods in agreement. "Straight from the source?"

Evie makes small whimpering sounds as I wade toward the edge again. The three of us prick our fingers, using claws, teeth, whatever we need to.

"Open up, little monster," Hess singsongs. I tilt Evie's head back and pull her bottom lip down with my thumb. We drip our blood in as one, careful not to give her too much.

"Swallow it down." I close her mouth, massaging her throat with my fingers. It bobs beneath my touch. We hold our breath, waiting for the blood to kick in. Its effects are almost instantaneous. Evie gasps, her eyes flying wide open. Her pupils dilate, turning the shimmering blues into a pitch-black void. She turns, pressing her lips against my mouth, completely unphased by the many razor-sharp fangs that lie just beneath my lips. Her body grinds against me and I chuckle. She whimpers when I gently pry her off.

"I need more." Her voice is husky and raw.

"I know, baby. But it's Reiner's turn now. Why don't we let him taste you?" I purr the words into her ear. She nods eagerly. I lift her out of the water and set her on the stony flat surface. Two of my tentacles encircle her legs, opening them wider. Another pair dips into her folds, spreading her pulsing, pink pussy wide for Reiner. His eyes zero in on her, tongue dipping out to wet his dark lips. He moves onto the boulder and drops to his knees, but stops his advance.

"Hess. Would you mind?" Reiner looks up uncertainly. Our bro is still so scared to hurt Evie.

"I've got you." Hess moves in close, hovering his hands over Evie's body. Heat radiates from his palms, warming Evie's little body. Bit by bit the water droplets that coat her fair skin evaporate. My tentacles don't love getting dried out in Hess's heat treatment, but I understand Reiner's concern. Water and electricity rarely go hand in hand. But he's a storm demon, for hell's sake. I know Reiner. He would never let his powers harm Evie. He just needs to learn to trust himself. "You're good to go, man." Hess claps him on the shoulder before stepping away.

Electricity flashes across Reiner's skin as he drops low. He's been getting brighter by the minute. The poor guy needs a release. He's just been too afraid to take it. I spread Evie wider, scooting her in Reiner's direction. He edges closer, lengthening his tongue. The first flick to Evie's skin makes her yelp. Reiner immediately pulls back.

"No." Evie reaches out, gripping Reiner by his horns and dragging him back between her thighs. "More, please."

Reiner slides his tongue up her center and her muscles jerk. She keeps her grip on his horns, and I'm grateful they don't seem to be conducting the same amount of energy as the rest of his body. The next lick up her seam has Evie moaning loudly.

"She loves it," Hess reassures him.

I reach my fingers down, toying with Evie's nipples while Reiner eats her out with increasing fervor. Sparks of energy pass between them and when Evie comes, I can feel the vibration of Reiner's power where my fingertips are grazing her skin.

Evie's arousal drips out, darkening the light gray stone beneath. Fuck, I want to drown in that. Reiner gains confidence, pushing a finger inside her. She spasms from the surge of energy but doesn't tell him to stop. Instead, she comes again almost right away. I have her held tightly in my arms, keeping her spread and supporting her while Reiner feasts. Hess's voice breaks through the panting and moans.

"Tell him, Evie."

"What?"

"Tell him," Hess commands. "I can hear it bouncing around in that dirty mind of yours. Use your words."

"Reiner"—she swipes her tongue out, wetting her lips— "will you fuck me?"

He tenses, sitting back on the ground. "I might hurt you."

She sighs, but then looks up sharply. "Fine. Then will you let me fuck *you*?" She smirks.

Damn our girl is clever. Hess and I lock gazes. "That's not a bad Idea." I lift Evie and jump out of the water. Hess takes hold of Reiner's shoulders, cursing at the sharp crack of energy that invades his palms as he forces him to lie back.

"Wait—" Reiner starts.

"Give our little monster what she needs," I tell him, adamant. I set Evie down so she's straddling his waist.

His cock hums with energy that I can sense from my place behind them. The head pulses with a purplish light. Evie grips it but snaps her hand back as it releases a powerful shock. Reiner's face falls.

"Let me." I reach down before Reiner can protest, gripping his cock. He groans, thrusting up into my tight fist. I love the way his shaft thrums against my fingers. His dark body and explosive powers are an irresistible storm of shadow and sin. Thinking of our first intimate experience makes me lick my lips. I was drawn to Reiner for years before he acknowledged his own feelings. When the two of us are together... Well, he enjoys my tentacles even more than Hess. A rush of excitement fills me. We have so much to share with Evie. But I won't focus on Reiner right now. Tonight is all about our girl.

I press his tip up into Evie. She cries out, her sweet voice singing to the heavens as she slides down over his thickness. Fuck, she looks incredible. Her head is thrown back as she slowly rolls her hips, taking him deeper and deeper.

Hess and I sit in revered silence, watching our girl ride Reiner's pulsing shaft like a demon queen. Every moment of this night feels surreal. I spent so long watching the others retrieve their brides. Wondering when it would be my turn. For the women who were gathered, it's felt like hours. One night of partying and fun. For the demons, it's been a time loop that's lasted years. None can leave until all have been gathered. The Shadowed One forbade us from revealing our true forms before all eleven brides had been brought together.

So the three of us waited—I would say patiently but that would be a lie—for a sign from the Shadowed One. The day we got the news that it was finally our time, I nearly wept. This is how it should be.

The sound of Evie coming undone for Reiner drags me out of my reminiscing. Reiner's current races through her, causing her lower abdomen to contract tightly enough that I can see the ridged outline of Reiner's dick as it pushes up inside her.

Hess steps closer, gripping his angry red shaft and looking like he's ready to burst. "Get her ready for me, Reiner."

Reiner's braided black tail emerges from beneath him. It sweeps behind Evie, and quickly unwinds, separating into three strands. Evie has picked up her pace and is riding Reiner's cock with a vengeful aura that has me wishing I were lying in his place. The tips of his tail drop to her lower back, sliding across her skin. I reach down, spreading her cheeks as one of the strands creeps lower. Evie sits upright, gasping as the first of the three tendrils dips inside. Her movements slow as she acclimates herself to the newest intrusion. Reiner slides the second tendril in, stretching her ass far wider than I dared to try with my single tendril.

"That's it," I extol. "We've got to loosen you up so that Hess will be able to fit his big cock in there."

Evie's gaze snaps up to Hess. "You're going to…" She sucks in a breath as Reiner presses the two deeper.

"That's right, little monster. I told you I'd have every part of that sweet body. I'm nothing if not a demon of my word." Hess circles behind her and I move to Reiner's front, giving him space.

"We've all enjoyed you in our own ways, but we've been holding back, Evie, darling." I plant my feet next to Reiner's head, angling my cock toward Evie's face.

"Some of the other couples have already finished," Hess whispers to Evie. "Let's give them a show."

Reiner grunts his approval from below. "It's time for everyone to see just how perfect you are for the three of us."

Chapter 5
Evie

Can this possibly be real? Did I fall and hit my head on the way to the Halloween party? Maybe someone drugged my drink and I'm hallucinating. Because if this night is real...

Reiner bucks up beneath me, sending a surge of prickly electric energy dancing through my core. I shift my hips, the charge of tingling flesh nearly too powerful, only to encounter the press of his tail moving deeper into my ass. *Okay, this feels real.*

One minute I'm being saved by a handsome stranger and introduced to his gorgeous friends, the next minute they're transforming into demons and threatening to triple-stuff me like I'm a fucking Oreo. Reiner adds the third length of his tail to my ass, making me cry out.

"Let him in, little monster." Hess's breath is warm against my ear. "Come for Reiner. Let him have you once more before we join." Hess's hands wrap around my hips, helping me to ride Reiner's cock again. I move awkwardly at first. The tails are filling me in a way I'm not used to. Each time I roll my hips, the burning stretch makes me hesitate. "Faster," Hess commands. I move faster, letting his grip on my waist help me to push past the uncomfortable new sensation. Hess bends over me, dropping his hands to my upper thighs and pressing my body down flush against Reiner's pelvis.

"What are you doing?" I pant out.

"Don't stop." His deep voice sends a shudder through me. "Let her have it, Reiner."

What starts as a simple tingling turns into a full-blown buzzing vibration that covers the entirety of Reiner's skin. It simmers into my flesh where it's pressed against his. My clit is immediately overstimulated, and I fight to pull back, to put some distance between my sensitive flesh and Reiner's vibrating skin. Hess keeps his hands firmly on my thighs, holding me in place.

"You can take it," Luda encourages, his fingers toying with my nipples.

The vibrations grow strong enough to rock through my center and make my teeth buzz. The moment between discomfort and bliss drops over me like a sun shower. One second I'm fighting to break free, the next I'm screaming out as a deep, sinful climax has me clenching tightly around Reiner's shaft and tail. *Air, breathing, lungs.*

Breathe, Evie, I have to remind myself. The moment my orgasm finishes, the vibrating sensation subsides. My muscles are sore and spent from so many orgasms in such little time, but at least my body has started to acclimate to the size and thickness of Reiner. In both places. I drop my hands to his chest, breathing heavily.

"That's our good girl," Reiner praises. He drags his tail out of me and I exhale in relief. A burning heat against my back signals Hess has dropped down behind me. He settles his weight on either side of Reiner's thighs, and I swallow nervously.

"Let's get you nice and wet." Hess lifts my hips up off Reiner, guiding him free from my throbbing pussy, and sliding his shiny, cum-covered cock between my cheeks several times. The feeling of wet arousal coating my sore backside makes me shiver. Hess lifts me up, pressing Reiner's tip back into my still-dripping entrance, and guides me back down, making me take Reiner to the hilt. "Lean forward and try to relax."

His hot palms press into my upper back, bending me forward. Reiner's clawed fingers wrap around my waist, stroking softly as Hess takes up position behind me. He was right about one thing. Several of the other couples have stopped fucking, and now have all eyes on us. A thrill lights up my center. I never realized being watched was a turn-on for me, but I find myself humming with excitement.

The press of Hess's tip against my tight hole has my focus switching back to my trio of monstrous men. He rubs his tip in circles, pressing a little more firmly but not penetrating. My eyes bulge. *How the hell am I going to take this?*

"Focus on me," Reiner says, his voice rumbling through the places where we're connected. He pulls my face toward his, exposing me even more to Hess. His dark lips find mine, locking our mouths together. I respond to the kiss tentatively, careful to avoid the sharpened teeth that I'm so unaccustomed to. My lips tingle. It reminds me of my favorite peppermint lip balm. *That's what Reiner smells like!* I've been trying to place his unusual scent. Mint, woods, and something endlessly shadowed.

Hess pulls my cheeks apart and I tense. The first inch of his thick head enters me. My throat catches, issuing a choked sound that Reiner swallows with his deadly kiss. Reiner continues stroking my back and hips, kissing me, working to take my mind off the way Hess is filling me so full that I can't stand it.

"Fuckkk..." Hess hisses behind me as he seats himself fully inside. His cock is so warm against my tense walls. "So fucking tight."

Reiner is the first to move his hips, thrusting up from beneath me and making me release a guttural sound of surprise. Hess remains still, but he doesn't have to move. Each time Reiner rocks my body with a powerful thrust it presses my hips up and back, sending Hess deeper inside. My cries turn to moans as the two find a rhythm that has them both stroking parts of me that I didn't even know existed. Reiner moves faster, his lips matching his hips. I choke slightly as his long, thick tongue delves into my mouth and halfway down my throat. He's obviously getting carried away. My chokes grow louder, and I spasm trying to breathe.

"Let me have that pretty mouth, Reiner," Luda implores, licking his lips and palming his erection. "I think Evie needs a cock in every hole."

Reiner's tongue slides out of my throat and I gasp for air. It's impossible to catch my breath with the two of them driving into me in unison. Luda's fingers grip my chin as he kneels to the right of Reiner's face.

His thigh brushes Reiner's cheek as he lines himself up. "Take a deep breath and open wide."

I do exactly as he commands. I'm already so full, but I can't help but lean into the desire to please him, to please all of them. My lips part, allowing Luda's unique cock to slide inside. The raised circular areas lining his head and shaft tickle the back of my throat as he glides deep enough to make me gag. And then he thrusts, making me cry out around him.

He's so big, so thorough in the way he's fucking my face, I find it impossible to swallow. Saliva drips from my mouth, rolling down Luda's shaft and coating his balls. Tears prick my eyes, blurring my vision as his thrusts become more forceful. I've never been more uncomfortable, and yet, I've never been more aroused. The feeling of being used by all three men has more of my seemingly endless arousal dripping down Reiner's shaft.

They continue their brutal pace, Hess and Reiner taking my ass and cunt while Luda drives himself down my throat. I'm gagging, drooling, tears running down my face. "You've never looked more fucking beautiful," Luda grits out, burying his fingers in my hair to give himself better leverage.

Reiner's skin buzzes to life, sending tingling energy all throughout me. Hess and Luda groan in pleasure and I know they can feel it too. My climax pushes out of me from all directions, my muscles unsure where or what to do with so many foreign intrusions. I scream my release with Luda's cock stuffing my mouth. My body tightens from the back of my throat to the tips of my toes. Hess is the first to come with me. His release is hot and welcome as it fills my ass. The heat seeps through me, and when it reaches Reiner's shaft he simpers with pleasure. His hips piston up into me with more force than before and seconds later I feel the rushing flow of his cum emptying into my pulsing center.

Luda is last. My jaw is burning from the unending stretch of him. He drives my face down, his eyes falling closed as his salty, warm spend pours into my eager mouth. I choke it down without thought, my body taking every bit of what he's giving me. I would have never swallowed for Sean. I wouldn't have let him do half the things these monsters have done. But it didn't take long to realize there isn't anything I wouldn't do to please my three demons.

I sigh in relief as he slides out from between my lips. I move to close my mouth but he catches it first, pressing his fingers into the soft flesh of my jaw. "Open wide, tongue out. I want to make sure you swallowed every last drop."

I ignore the ache and open my mouth wider, giving him a view down my raw throat. Luda leans forward, lengthening his tongue and massaging it along mine. He gives an inhuman sound of satisfaction as he tastes the remnants of his own release.

"Good little monster."

Hess carefully withdraws from my ass before lifting me up off Reiner's cock and into his strong, warm arms. I nuzzle into his heated red flesh, breathing in that spicy scent that's pure Hess.

"You were perfect," he whispers, leaning down to press a blistering kiss to my lips.

I purr as he passes me into the cool creek water where Luda's arms are outstretched for me. Luda cleans me up, using gentle strokes to get as much demon cum off and out of me as he can. The cold water feels heavenly on my swollen sex. When he's finished, he passes me back to Hess, who heats me until I'm dry and then sets me on my feet.

Reiner lifts my arms, sliding his black t-shirt over my head. The fabric drops to mid-thigh, shielding my body. Once I'm covered, Hess swoops me up, and we make our way back to the bonfire. The others have all finished their sexual endeavors and covered the girls up in some form of clothing or half-torn Halloween costume. There's a warm energy flowing through my veins. I see it reflected on the faces of the others.

Hess slides me into Reiner's lap before standing to address the group. "Our blood will be wearing off soon. It was a temporary sensation, but if you choose to stay with us, rest assured, it will be yours permanently. Every woman in this group is more valuable than the air in our lungs, or powers in our demon forms. If you stay with us, your existence will become pure pleasure and love. You were chosen for us, and there's not a monster here who wouldn't give their lives for you in a mortal heartbeat."

That was a little intense.

"What do you mean stay with you?" Georgia cocks an eyebrow from her position wrapped up in Kodi's six arms.

"Yeah, this was incredible, but..." Cami chews her lip.

"But we have lives to get back to. Families, responsibilities," I add, feeling as if I'm speaking for all of us. Part of me hasn't even been able to accept that this is real. The rest of the girls nod and murmur their agreement. The men exchange silent glances. When Hess turns to me again, there's a sadness in his eyes that has my chest tightening.

"No, you don't."

Dread creeps up my spine. We don't have families? Responsibilities? "What does that mean? You're going to keep us here? If you're worried about your secrets, I'm sure the others—"

"You died, Evie."

"I—" My stomach caves in like I've been punched. I open my mouth to speak but can't seem to find the right words. "No."

Hess sighs, and crouches down so he's level with my eyes. He takes my hands in his, his thumbs stroking gently. "I didn't save you from the crash. I wasn't helping you to recover from the shock. I was holding you as you took your last breath."

The broken look in his gaze brings tears to my eyes. I want to protest, but a memory flashes through my mind so potent and powerful that it nearly drags me under. Headlights, impact, my arms, legs, and lungs failing to work. My terror. The soothing words of Hess as I...as I... "I died." Tears stream freely down my face.

"You all did," Kodi speaks from across the fire. Stunned looks radiate around the group. My gaze falls to Georgia. Her face is pale, her eyes wide with horror.

"I jumped?" she whispers. Kodi nods, his silver eyes filled with pain. The news story from several years back comes flooding to the forefront of my mind and suddenly I can see it so clearly. *Georgia Dawson. Jumped to her death from the top of the Ferris wheel at the Sugar Hill Halloween carnival. She was only twenty-five.*

"Wait." Cami's breaths are coming quick and shallow. "That means…" She brushes the hair from in front of her face, her fingertips sliding just beneath her eye. The shimmering blue iris fades to a lifeless milky white before returning to its usual color. It means Ethan didn't save her from getting shot after all. Anger rises inside my chest. I hope that psychotic ex of hers is rotting in jail. Or better yet, in the ground. Ethan pulls her into his massive, navy chest as her cries come loudly.

"We can't all have died on the same day." Dawn is shaking her head violently. "That isn't possible."

"You didn't," Abbot answers. "Sonja was the first. She passed nearly fifteen years ago. The rest of you came scattered over the Halloweens throughout the years that followed."

Sonja stands, her body shaking with rage. "Did you cause our deaths?"

"No." Rhylan grips her arm, pulling her into his body. "You were assigned to us, chosen by the Shadowed One. We patiently waited, biding our time here. It had to be your natural time to pass." He gestures to the bonfire and the ruins. "We waited and waited until each of you passed in the way that was meant for your life path. We couldn't interfere. We couldn't take you sooner, or even stop your deaths."

"But, I just got here. It's only been a few hours. My family, my sisters…" Sonja's voice is frantic.

Rhylan shakes his head. "For you, it's been fifteen years." He strokes her hair as silent tears trail down her cheeks.

"What is this place?" I ask, finally finding my voice.

"This is an in-between. A place of holding between our world and yours, where time passes differently." Hess gazes so deeply into my eyes it makes my heart hurt.

A moth flutters out of the mist, landing on my bare knee. Several others emerge, all finding perches on some part of the girls.

"The Death's-head moths are spirit guides. They escort souls from one plane to the next," Reiner says quietly, resting his hand near the moth and allowing it to climb onto his finger. "That's why there are so many gathered here. They've waited a long time hoping to help you move on."

"There is a place"—Luda's voice is softer than before—"one where the dead from your world usually go. But there is another path for you."

Hess strokes my skin. "You can follow the moths, cross over as was intended. Or, you can come with us, to our realm."

"And be ours forever," Luda adds, placing his hand on my lap. My gaze shifts to the other couples. They're all speaking in hushed voices with the girls in their arms.

"You were chosen, divinely selected to be brides for the demons of our realm. One, or two in Abbot's case, for every main species we have. We'll never look human again, but if you choose us, I swear to you you'll be so loved. You'll be treated like a queen for all eternity." Hess swallows thickly, his burning eyes reflecting my broken heart back at me. "Come home with us, Evie. We've waited ages to find you. Be ours. Let us take care of you."

I'm breathless as I soak this all in. There's a deep ache in my heart that I now realize is no longer beating. Anger, hurt, betrayal, confusion, denial all war within my hollow ribcage. If it's the truth...if my life really is over and I have the choice to leave, or to be with them. "You'll share me? Like the twins with Sonja?" They nod in unison. "Oh god, are you brothers?" A sudden wave of nausea swirls through my gut at the memory of Luda sucking Hess's cock.

Luda practically cackles. "We are not related. We just happen to be the same species. Where some others have one family in charge of things, our particular kingdom has three."

I mull that information over. "So you're like, some sort of demon princes?"

They nod. It's a lot of information. Too much for my fuzzy brain to absorb.

"I know it's a lot," Hess whispers apologetically.

The number of moths grows as I sit in silence, trying to digest everything they've told me. There must be hundreds of them now, covering the ground and hovering in the air. I take another resigned breath, wondering if I even need air anymore. "I really died?"

Hess wraps his warm arms around me. "Yes. But if you come with us, you'll never need to worry about death again. You'll want for nothing, need nothing. We'll worship you day and night. We want nothing more than to give you all the happy possibilities that were stolen from you upon death's reaping."

"Time's almost up," Reiner murmurs. I follow his gaze to where the sun has just begun to peek above the tree line. "If we don't go now, you won't be able to pass through until the veil thins again next Halloween."

"What will it be, Evie?" Luda's green eyes are wide with hope.

"Ours for Halloween?" Hess asks.

I'm scared, uncertain, unwilling to accept the truth. Even so, I trust these three with my life. Or death, I suppose. I can't explain it, but this moment just feels right.

"Yours forever," I answer, giving them a soft sad smile.

Three sets of arms close in around me. Their relief is nearly tangible in the air. Two massive trees shudder nearby, twisting and bending to create a wide archway. Warm light spills through from the other side. Georgia and Kodi are the first to pass through. Their bodies vanish into the ethereal glow.

Sonja and the twins are next, followed by Cami and Ethan. The remaining couples follow suit, until all ten have passed into the light.

The four of us tread quietly toward the woodland arch. I stop just before it, my chest a mangled flurry of energy and anticipation. Luda takes my right hand. Reiner takes my left. Hess moves close behind me, circling his arms around my waist.

I say goodbye. To everything I was. Releasing my old life and casting my memories to be carried away on the wings of the moths. A lightness and warmth spread through the holes where such sadness once resided. My three men peer down at me, anxiously awaiting my next move.

I sigh in contentment, stepping forward. "Let's go home."

Epilogue

The sound of the garage door screeching open has my pulse racing. I would have taken care of this sooner, but Evie insisted on being a part of it. That meant we had to wait. In time, she'll be able to cross between worlds without issue. For now, she can only enter this realm when the veil is at its thinnest.

I mold myself to the shadows as the busted-up red Bronco rolls into the small garage. My gaze fixes on the large dent on the front bumper. A queasiness lurches through me. It's quickly replaced by unbridled rage. *He didn't even bother to get it fixed.*

The piece of shit himself stumbles out of the driver's side, not even trying to hide the half-empty liquor bottle in his fist. He treks around behind his car, having parked too close to the wall to pass in front of it. A group of small, costumed children abandon ringing his doorbell and run up to him as soon as he comes into view.

"Trick or treat!" they call out in excited, childish voices.

"Fuck off, you little shits," he yells at them, making several of the children jump before running away into the night.

My gaze follows Floyd Scheuer as he limps toward the button to close the garage. We've learned so much about him in the short time since we arrived. I was hit with an immense wave of dark energy when we first portaled in. After a quick exploration of the property, we found the source. Bodies. At least a dozen. Some had been damaged so badly it was hard to tell which bones belonged to who. Floyd isn't some accidental drunk driver. He's a predator. The most recent grave we found belonged to a girl the same age as Evie. She went missing last Halloween. Did he take her after he hit Evie? Was she already buried in the ground by the time he murdered our girl? The darkness swirling around the poor girl's shallow grave was filled with torment and pain. Whatever he did to her, to all those girls, it was horrific enough to leave an energetic imprint in this realm. Evie was lucky to go the way she did.

Most of the people in the mortal world would call us monsters. But Floyd is a true devil. If he had gotten his hands on Evie that night...

My rage builds. We're going to make sure he never hurts another girl again.

He slams a fist against the illuminated square and the garage creaks back closed. His hand inches toward the doorknob and anticipation prickles beneath my skin.

"Mother fuck!" he screams, yanking his hand away from the knob and clutching it to his chest. He lowers his arm, staring down at the blistered flesh in utter confusion. I grin. *Well done, Hess.* Floyd's gaze flicks between his burnt palm, the sliver knob, and the liquor bottle in his other hand. He begrudgingly sets his liquor on the floor and reaches for the door again.

His screams sound even better the second time. This hand looks even worse. The bubbled skin has already popped, revealing raw, sizzling flesh beneath the open wounds. He cries out, reaching for the button that opens the garage door. I slam my palm against the wall, sending electricity racing across space. It fries the power, and the illuminated button dims before going out completely. Floyd curses as he's plunged into complete darkness. I step out of the shadows, releasing a low growl. Floyd's cursing ceases. His breathing picks up. He's just realized he is not alone.

"Who's there?" he bellows, fear causing his voice to rise in pitch. None of us speak. I don't need to hear the others to know they're on the move. I can sense them closing in on our prey. I line myself up behind our target, waiting for Hess to move in.

A flame flickers to life, illuminating Hess's twisted red features. "Boo."

Floyd screams, stumbling backwards. In his haste to escape Hess he comes crashing into my open arms. I flood his body with electricity, relishing the way his muscles seize up before falling limp. He passes out even quicker than I expected.

"You better not have killed him already," Luda chastises as he's revealed by the glow of the flames in Hess's palm.

"I didn't," I snap back.

"Are you sure?" Luda smirks at me. My fingers land on Floyd's pulse point, double-checking. He's still alive. *For now.*

"He's going to wish his death had been as quick and merciful as my electric shocks."

"Shit, Reiner. I love it when you're unhinged. I thought Evie might have made you go soft." Luda teases.

I grunt in response. I can't deny that Evie has done a number on me. She's tamed my monster, for the most part. But there are certain circumstances that have me regressing to the heartless demon I was the first hundred years or so of my life. It never ceases to amaze me how often people assume that my being the quietest makes me the least dangerous. Of the three of us, I have the highest penchant for violent tendencies—when the appropriate occasion arises. Today is one such occasion.

Hess lights several more fires, they hover in the air, illuminating the garage. Luda and I haul Floyd into a chair and tie him up. We stare down at him, waiting.

"Damn dude, how much longer is this going to take?" Luda whines. He has no patience. Everything in his life is about instant gratification.

I can't deny my own eagerness. I send another shock into Floyd's arm and he jumps awake. The sounds of his panicked screams immediately fill the space.

"Someone shut him up," Hess growls.

I oblige his request, using one of my lengthened talons to slice off the fingers on his left hand. His screams build to an unbearable volume before I stuff the severed digits into his mouth, muffling the sounds. Blood pours from his maimed hand.

"We don't want you to bleed out before the fun starts." Hess stalks closer, gripping the fingerless nub and cauterizing it.

"Well done." Luda claps.

"It's time. Go get her," I breathe. Hess vanishes, portaling back home and leaving a puff of smoke in his wake.

I circle Floyd, glaring down at him. "Do you know what day it is?" Tears stream down his cheeks as he shakes his head. "It's an anniversary of sorts. Today, we celebrate the day the most important woman in the world fell into our clutches." I drag a claw along his cheek and he thrashes against his binds. "It's also the anniversary of your unspeakable crime. And the day you atone for it."

The room heats, signaling Hess's return. Floyd's eyes bulge as he stares at the newcomer. "Remember me?" Evie strolls out of the shadows, looking like a true queen.

The first few weeks after her arrival into our world were spent filling her full of as much of our blood and cum as we could. The blood was to help sustain her while her body acclimated to the demon realm. The cum, well that was just because we couldn't help ourselves. The changes in her appearance were subtle at first. The inky glow in her blue irises, the sharpening of her fingernails. She took her true demon form the day the twin, opalescent horns spiraled up from the top of her skull. Those additions have been most enjoyable. I love the way she squirms when I run my tongue up and down the smooth, bony spires. I can make her come from that alone. Of course, she has her own hold on the rest of us when it comes to horns. The second she sucks our horns between her plump lips, we become mindless beasts of pleasure, simpering at her lovely feet.

She moves gracefully toward the parked car, her midnight-blue dress flowing behind her with ethereal beauty. Her ivory, clawed fingers slide along the large dent, and my insides tighten. "Looks about my size, don't you think?"

Floyd's eyes gleam in that way humans always do when a lightbulb comes on. "He remembers you now," Hess snarls.

"That's good." Evie smiles, her beautiful features at odds with the dark situation. "I like the space you've chosen, boys. But it's missing something." She looks around, tapping a sharp tip on her chin.

"What does it need, little monster?" Hess draws her close, running his fingers through her long hair.

Evie's eyes settle on Floyd, and I watch as darkness seeps into her sparkling gaze. "To be painted red."

Fuck. My cock hardens at her words. The others groan, and I know they're feeling the same effects.

I strike without hesitation. My claws rake across his cheek, digging deep enough to reveal the fingers stuffed inside his mouth. Blood flings from my fingertips as they sweep past. Hess attacks next, driving his horns into Floyd's stomach and wrenching upwards. A mass of blood and guts splatters across the room. At this rate, our victim will be dead in no time.

Luda drags Evie into his arms. "Come here, baby. We don't want to get your pretty dress dirty." He slips the straps of her dress off, allowing the gown to drop down around her feet like a puddle of silky blue water. My gaze devours the sight of her bare, pale body. Luda moves her closer. Hess and I exchange a look, knowing exactly what he wants us to do.

The next time my claws slash through the murdering son of a bitch's chest, I aim my fingers forward, growling in satisfaction as the blood splashes across Evie's milky skin. Hess follows suit, sending another blast of arterial spray exploding in Evie's direction.

Evie gasps with each spray. Luda takes up position behind her, running his hands along her body, smearing the blood across her throat and full breasts. He spreads the dripping red mess lower, cupping Evie's perfect sex. Luda circles in front of her, dropping to his knees. Evie's hands fly to his horns. She hooks one thigh over Luda's shoulder as he licks the blood from her pussy. Her first moan of ecstasy has us ripping into the monster beneath us like absolute animals. Her luminous blue eyes never leave us. We throw ourselves into the task at hand. Blood flings around the room, continuing to color Evie red. She releases a feral growl that has us all rock hard, then kicks out at Luda, knocking him flat on his back. She climbs astride his chin, straddling him and taking his tongue deep inside. Our girl really is perfect. Electricity ricochets through my body as I watch her ride Luda's face. What I wouldn't give to be in his shoes right now. She rolls her hips, grinding against him and screaming as her first climax hits. The sound of her coming undone is a sexy song she sings just for us.

It takes me longer than it should to realize Evie's murderer has been dead for several minutes. Damn. I wanted to see the life drain from his eyes. Now that I look closer, I realize he doesn't have any eyes. Was that Hess's doing or mine? Movement in my peripherals catches Hess striding toward our girl. He grips one of her horns, jerking her head back and taking her lips in a bloody and vicious kiss. She rises without warning, pulling Hess closer and guiding his legs to either side of Luda's head.

"Kneel," she commands. Hess drops without question. Evie strokes Hess's cock, guiding it to Luda's lips. I don't think she'll ever get enough of those two. Hess fucks Luda's face without hesitation. They both moan, lost in passion. Evie turns her attention toward me. Her feet splash through the puddles of blood as she makes her way around the chair. My tongue lengthens, running along her neck and nipples. She turns her back to me, leaning over the slumped, unrecognizable corpse still tied to the chair. "Touch me, Reiner."

I push up behind her, giving her my cock in one punishing thrust. My gaze travels to where Hess is pistoning his hips into Luda's throat. Something new dawns on me. *She's recreating our first night together.*

"You're a bad, bad girl," I growl into her ear, picking up my pace and delivering a jolt of electricity into her core. She's quickly lost to the bliss of my buzzing electricity between her thighs. Neither of us pays much attention to the mangled body as the power of my thrusts dislodges it from the chair. The remaining pieces of Floyd Scheuer hit the floor with a wet plop. I barely hear it. Evie's screams of pleasure are filling my ears. The thrill of the kill has me worked up and ready to come the first time Evie's walls clamp down around me. I roar in frustration, not wanting this to end so soon, but eventually give in to the primal need to fill her with my seed. Evie pushes her hips back, milking me until I'm tender and twitching.

She's breathing heavily, but I know that wasn't nearly enough to satisfy our girl. I pick her up, her body slippery and wet in my grasp. I close the distance between us and the others. "On your feet," I command Luda and Hess. Hess stops his thrusting with a groan, moving to his feet and dragging Luda up with him. I set Evie down between them, turning her to face Hess. He lifts her up, hooking his arms beneath her thighs. Evie barely has a second to come to her senses before Hess has his big cock buried in her freshly fucked cunt. Luda is quick to slide in behind her. He smears more of the blood down her back, using it to lubricate her ass. His deep, green cock slides in, making Evie's eyes roll back in her head.

They seesaw her, sliding her back and forth on their dicks in a well-practiced rhythm. I enjoy watching them like this, but I know Evie likes it when all three of us participate. I use my right hand to grip one of Hess's copper horns. My left hand clutches an ivory horn of Luda's. My tongue slinks out, wrapping around one of Evie's pearly spirals. I tighten my grip on all three, and then begin to stroke. The sounds they make have me quickening my pace.

Evie's hand shoots out, strangling my cock and pulling me closer. I thrust into her grip, losing myself to the veil of lust hanging heavy over our group. The four of us fuck, stroke, and lick, every part of each other. We're dark, depraved, covered in blood, and so goddamn in love it's sickening.

Evie's screams are all of our undoing. Her body tightens, throat running raw as she orgasms with a dark demonic howl. Luda and Hess come in the same moment, their bodies pumping Evie full of cum. I follow shortly after, my spend spurting out of me and coating Evie's body. The three of us slow our thrusts as we ride our communal high.

My mind is filled with post-orgasmic clouds, but through the fuzz I'm still able to recognize how truly lucky we are. The wait was long and torturous, but Evie was worth every moment of fear and doubt.

Evie sighs then giggles. "I don't think my dress made it through the carnage." The dress in question has been reduced to a sopping, bloodstained pile of fine fabrics.

"Thats alright, we prefer you naked," I tease.

Evie's joyous expression sobers as her eyes land on Floyd's corpse. "Burn this place to the ground, Hess. And then let's go home."

Flames rise up from every corner of the room. We left the many backyard graves uncovered. When the police investigate the fire and search the property, they'll find those girls. A knot loosens in my chest. Tonight will bring peace and resolution to more than just our girl. Hess portals us out just as his crimson fire engulfs the corpse, car, and any evidence of our being here.

My heart lightens as we close this chapter of our lives. Floyd Scheuer was a loose end that had been nagging at my soul for months. Killing him set us all free. He was a murderer, but without him, we never would have gotten our Evie.

Too bad I forgot to thank him.

Evie

Home. My refuge. The demon realm feels more like heaven than I would have thought possible. I stand on the balcony of our sleek, black castle. It was built on the edge of the three-way divide that lines each of the royal family's lands. The smoky, fire-filled landscape of Hess lies to my right. Luda's raging, emerald sea sits sparkling to my left. And the endless storm of Reiner's people rests just before me. I spend hours here, watching the lightning arc through the dark clouds.

Hess's spicy scent alerts me to his presence even before he speaks. "Did you enjoy your Halloween?" His warm hand lands on my shoulder.

I giggle. "Oh yes, the murder and orgy were both spectacular."

"Did someone say orgy?" Luda slides into my peripherals, taking a seat next to me.

"Is that all you think about?" Reiner grumbles, striding out to join us.

"It is around Evie." Luda gives me a mischievous wink.

Watching the three of them interact fills my heart with a love like nothing I experienced in the mortal world.

Hess leans forward, wrapping his arms around me. "I have to admit it was my favorite part."

"Mine too. Oh, and the babies loved their first taste of blood. They wouldn't stop kicking for hours after." The air around me falls absolutely silent.

"Babies?" Hess flaps his great wings, flying overhead and landing before me. I nod, my smile growing wider by the second.

We weren't sure how long it would take for me to be able to conceive. My body needed time to transition from human to demon. But I woke up one morning many months ago and knew without a doubt that there was life within me. More than one. I can't get a reading on just how many, but I think it's two. Keeping it a secret may have been the hardest thing I've ever done. I had to teach myself how to build a mental shield to keep Hess from discovering it before I wanted him to. The concealment spell was also a necessity. My growing belly would have triggered their suspicions. With how protective the three of them are, I knew they would have made me stay home tonight. And I wanted to be there to watch Floyd suffer. I drop the spell, allowing my growing bump to become visible.

"Evie!" Luda exclaims. All three have me wrapped up in a tight hug that nearly crushes me.

"We've got to tell the others." Hess is smiling wider than I've ever seen before. "Georgia and Cami are going to freak."

I let out a small huff, poking out my bottom lip. "It's so unfair Cami got wings." The redheaded beauty sprouted a pair of crimson, feathery wings that are nearly as large as Hess's.

"You are perfect without wings," Reiner mumbles, stroking my back.

"Let's invite everyone over," Luda exclaims. "Right now!"

Over the past year the other brides and I have grown so close. I'm grateful for my husbands, but also thankful I was blessed with so many beautiful new friends. We all experienced something unimaginable and came out the other side better than ever. We laugh, cry, taking turns at each other's castles, reminiscing over forbidden fruits and demon wine. I don't know what I would do without them.

"Calm down, Luda. They're probably all out in the mortal world for Halloween." Hess shakes his head.

"The twins are going to be so pissed that we got our girl knocked up first." Luda rubs his hands together excitedly.

I give him a smack on the arm. "Don't say it like that. 'Knocked up' sounds so crass."

"And the things you let us do to you aren't crass?" Hess whispers in my ear.

"I have no idea what you're talking about." I feign innocence.

Reiner drags me into his arms and heads toward the bedroom. "Let us jog your memory."

My spirit brightens and my soul sings. The four of us are an odd bunch, but the Shadowed One knew exactly what they were doing when we were chosen for each other. I take a contented breath, smiling until my cheeks hurt. Three big demons and two littles on the way. A slight kick has my hand dropping low to my belly. The others notice and start shoving each other, fighting to get their hands on my stomach. Our family is growing.

My gaze moves from one of my monstrous men to the next. Hess, Luda, and Reiner. How perfect they are. My darkly depraved monsters.

Bonus Scene

Luda

"And what if I wanted front-row seats to the dynastic storm too?" I huff out.

"We agreed tonight was *my night* alone with Evie," Reiner growls.

Evie finishes buttoning her pale-yellow gown and turns to me with a glare. "Don't start this again. We all agreed on the schedule. Everyone gets their date night. You had yours just three nights ago." She cocks an eyebrow at me. "Or have you forgotten our celebration of the rising of the emerald moon so soon?"

Oh, I most certainly have not forgotten. The emerald moon is like a shot of pure power into the veins of us water demons. It only happens once every two hundred years. I worked Evie with my tentacles and cock for nearly four delicious hours beneath the verdant glow of the full moon. Her body squirmed and squirted, over and over for me, within the dark waters of the sparkling sea. I'm certainly grateful for her demon transformation. Otherwise, she'd never be able to withstand the number of hours and ways the three of us bend her body to our twisted wills.

I fold my arms and grin. "I suppose you're right. I'd like to see Reiner top that experience."

"Trust me, I have plenty of devious acts in store for Evie. She'll have forgotten all about your little moon party by the end of the night." Reiner glows as he allows electricity to arc across his dark skin.

I stick my lip out in a pout. Evie just giggles, rushing over to me. "It's one night. And you know I prefer all of you equally." She leans up on her toes, waiting. I dip down, taking her mouth in a feverish kiss that leaves her breathless and grinning.

She moves to Hess next, kissing him and whispering in his ear. Hess looks even more unhappy than I feel. He returns her kiss before storming away down one of the many castle halls.

"You two." Evie shakes her head. "I'll be back before you know it." She gives me a wink and something inside me melts.

I wander aimlessly after the two take their leave. No point in seeking out Hess. He's been terribly grumpy lately. I think I'll spend my evening in the grotto.

My trek to the grotto leads me deep beneath the castle. A stone stairwell opens up into the greenish-blue space that houses my sanctuary. The air is salty and damp. My tentacles begin to unfurl, sensing the presence of the incandescent liquid. I glide into the cool pool, sighing as my body blends seamlessly into its water form.

Hours pass in a blink down here. The mineral-rich water brightens my scales and soothes my spirit. I float on my back, eyes closed, listening to the sounds of the water. There aren't any windows to the outside world here, but I'd guess we're already well into nightfall. It shouldn't be too long now. Evie and Reiner's date can't last more than a few hours. Of course, I know all too well how easy it is to get carried away when we're with our girl.

The sharp uptick in temperature alerts me to Hess's presence. *There goes my peaceful evening.* I open my eyes, finding a scowling Hess towering over the edge. "Miss me?" I taunt, swimming closer.

"Where the hell are they?" he growls. Hess is only days away from his annual fire molt. The blazing color beneath his skin makes that obvious. By the end of the week, his body will have engulfed itself in flames and reformed with even more power than before. It's how fire demons keep their magic flowing and growing. The side effect of this phenomenon is a temporary increase in aggression and temper. It only lasts a few days, but Hess is as hotheaded as demonly possible the whole time.

My mouth quirks up in a smirk. "Who are we speaking of?"

Smoke curls up from around Hess's nose and lips. "You know damn well."

"Need Evie to quell your roid rage?" I tease.

Hess's copper eyes blaze. He needs a release. That much is painfully clear. "Come closer." His tone leaves no room for argument. Anticipation sizzles though me. My cock twitches as he curls a finger, beckoning me forward. I'm a sucker for Hess when he's all hot and bothered. I reach the edge and stand, bringing myself level to Hess's waist. He strokes his thickening shaft. The red veins pulse with life beneath his eager touch. "Open your mouth."

A drop of thick precum pools on the crimson tip. My tongue darts out, swiping across my lips as desire surges through me. Hess groans as he watches the motion. His hips press forward, angling his erection closer to my face. Usually, I would give in without a fight. But I'm in a playful mood. Hess is used to being the one in charge. The one who can so easily dominate our bodies and minds.

Not today.

I'm going to give him a taste of his own medicine— My tentacles shoot out, wrapping around his thick neck— *with every inch of my cock down his throat...*

Hess releases a gasp of surprise as I jerk hard, forcing him down to his knees. "Luda—" he starts, but I tighten my grip on his neck.

I let a free tentacle trail up and down his abdomen, gliding it to the base of his burning shaft and circling it once. He thrusts his hips forward, but I withdraw my hold just as quickly. It earns me another unhappy growl. "You've been unbearably bossy these past few days, ordering us around, forcing us to withstand your outbursts, making the air practically boil." The water bubbles around me as I summon it, using it to raise me higher until I'm lined up with Hess's jaw. "I think it's time for you to apologize."

Hess's eyes go wide, then darken. "You may get what you want now but mark my words, Luda"—the tip of his forked tongue teases out, swiping up my precum—"you are going to be in so much trouble later..."

By the gods that tongue is so warm. I need more. I pull him firmly toward me, pressing my throbbing tip against his lips. Heat races up my spine as Hess's warm mouth envelops me. The stark contrast in our body temperatures has me shivering with pleasure. My tentacles flex out of instinct, their suckers massaging every place they make contact with Hess's skin and crawling out to grasp even more of him. He draws his lips into an *o* before sucking me deep into his throat. *Gods...* It's so good that I momentarily lose sight of the room around me. My eyes must have rolled into the back of my damn skull. The silky feel of Hess's talented tongue as he draws back has my hips jerking forward, desperate to be deep inside him once more. Hess chuckles, sensing my eagerness.

"What do you want, Luda?" He fights against my hold on him, peering up at me with fire-stained eyes. "Use your words."

Damn him. He's found a way to take some of his unbreakable control back. I frown down at him. "Fuck you. You know what I want." My hips press forward again, but he turns his face to the side, avoiding opening his mouth once more.

"Tell me." His voice echoes inside my mind, deep and sultry. His words bordering right on the edge of compulsion.

"Dammit, Hess," I growl, not enjoying that I've lost the edge of this dominant/submissive game we're playing. "Suck my cock," I grit out.

Hess tsks. *"Beg."*

Fuck. Why does that single word make me even harder? Hess knows exactly how to get under my skin and make me squirm for him. I try to overtake him by force once more, using my tentacles to drag him closer. That fiery bastard fights back, always keeping a breath away from where I need him most. His strength has always been so attractive to me. Now it seems it will be my downfall. My hands drop to his horns and stroke. It's my last bargaining chip. "Suck my cock. Please. *Please.* Choke me down. Swallow my cum. I'm fucking begging you." I practically sob those last few words. My erection is stiff, painful.

Hess practically howls as I pump the length of his copper spires. He dives forward, swallowing the length of my cock so unexpectedly that if it weren't for the water holding me up my knees would have buckled. His hot, wet lips squeeze my length while his wicked tongue swirls up and down my shaft. The combination stops my breath.

My cockhead hits the back of his throat and I gasp, replenishing the air in my lungs. My moans shatter the stoic silence of the grotto, creating an endless audible loop of pleasure and depravity. My grip on Hess's horns tightens. Something warm and sticky rubs against my ankle. The next time Hess pulls back to the tip, I peer down. His hard, red cock bobs with need. It brushes against my scaley skin before dripping more of his seed onto the damp floor below.

I wonder If I can make him come just by stroking his horns. Evie does it. With her soft, small hands. Mine are large, clawed. I spit on each horn, adding lubrication and gliding up and down in a rhythm that matches the sucking of Hess's devilish mouth. He groans around my cock, his hips rolling, thrusting into vacant air. My tentacles snake out without thought, wrapping around his thickness.

His hips buck forward and I grin. *I'm back in control.* My hold on his horns tightens as my tentacles squeeze him without mercy.

Hess's voice dances in my mind. *"You are a fool if you believe that to be true."* He drives down to the hilt, his lips kissing my pelvis. He swallows with my cock down his throat, his muscles constricting around me until I can't stand it. I climax, my cum rushing out of me in a violent spasm that has my spine practically bent in half. The second I release the last drop, Hess raises his body temperature. My tentacles shrink back in an instant as the fiery heat scalds their sensitive flesh.

Hess strikes the moment I release him.

My world spins as I'm flipped around and forced onto my hands and knees in the pool. Hess splashes in behind me, sending waves across the surface. The grotto fills with steam as Hess's heated skin reacts with the cool water.

Heat burns up against the backs of my thighs. "I told you you'd be in trouble."

Hess

Oh, Luda. What am I going to do with you? My body is taut with need as I drop to my knees behind him. The water reaches mid-thigh for us both. His gasp of surprise as I force him to submit is utterly satisfying. He may have enjoyed his little moment of control, but deep down he knows the truth. Everything that happened was only because I allowed it to happen.

It's not that I didn't enjoy it. On the contrary, pleasuring Luda brings me its own unique brand of satisfaction. He and I have a long history of finding all the ways we can make each other scream and squirm. We began indulging in our fantasies years before we found our Evie. Now, I'm looking forward to wringing moans from him until he's fallen silent from sheer bliss. Which will truly be a feat, considering Luda almost never stops talking.

The water sizzles around me, producing thick clouds of steam. It obscures my view and settles in my lungs. *This will not do.* I want to see Luda as I take his body and break his spirit. I flex my wings, sweeping them back and forth and clearing the air around us. Vibrant emerald scales shimmer into view. Luda truly is magnificent. I run my claws along his smooth spine. His back arches, tentacles flailing as they react to my touch. He looks so perfect like this, panting, helpless, desperate for my cock.

I lengthen my tongue fully. My mouth is still filled with moisture from sucking off Luda. Saliva drips from my forked tip, dribbling down and coating him. I spread him wide, making sure every bit is slick and ready to take me. I line my tip with his entrance, not needing to use my hands. My dick is so hard I could lift the fucking furniture. My hands wrap around the fronts of his thighs, making him jump.

"Do you still feel like the one in charge?" I nudge the head of my cock against his tight entrance and he sucks in a breath. "Or do you see now that I am your god and master?" I thrust into him, tightening my grip on his thighs to hold him in place. Luda cries out, but the sound is followed by a long, low moan. I love the way he takes me. His body is always so cool, so soft, so tight. I drag to the tip, allowing him one deep breath before plunging to the hilt. My eyes devour the way we look together. Iridescent green meets fiery red where our bodies connect. I sheath myself fully and still my movements. Luda chokes as I fill him so full he can barely stand it. He wriggles beneath me but I keep a firm hold on him.

"You're a bad, bad boy, Luda." I slam an open palm across the right side of his ass without warning. His body tightens as he yelps out. The feeling of him constricting around my engorged length is nearly indescribable. I spank him again, brightening the first handprint I left behind. He releases a gravelly moan. His knees struggle beneath me as he works to dislodge some of my massive length from within him. "Oh, you're not going anywhere." I press in even farther, removing any last bit of space between our flesh. "You're mine, Luda." I circle my hips, staying fully buried inside him. Luda throws his head back and howls. I watch with great satisfaction as his eyes roll back. The green of his irises momentarily disappears, revealing vacant white as his body short-circuits beneath my depraved assault. I lean forward, clutching his chin and whispering in his ear. "And after that little stunt you pulled tonight, you should have known better than to think I'd take it easy on you."

My next thrust is primal and rough. Luda's breaths come out ragged and heavy. "Hess..." he groans.

"You're mine, Luda. My needy little toy." I tilt my hips, reentering him at a new angle. I'm rewarded with a guttural moan of gratitude. I know his body. I know every filthy thing he likes. "I control your pleasure." I roll my hips, dragging to the tip and pressing back inside. "So, beg me for release. Beg me to fuck you."

"I need it. Please, Hess. Fuck me. Do it the way only you can."

I grin at his breathy praise. "As you wish."

My hips whip forward, picking up pace. Luda's moans come loud and unbidden. He's so vocal during sex. I fucking love it. One hand moves to his shoulder as I anchor us together. Every thrust, every snap of the hips melds our bodies into one writhing form. I'm lost in a dream, so lost that I don't feel the tentacle coming until it's too late. It slips inside me, making me gasp with pleasure. *Sneaky little—*

The slick appendage drives deeper, delivering me pleasure, matching the erotic dance I'm engaging in with Luda. Now it's my turn to moan. We lose ourselves to the desire overtaking our bodies and minds. Sounds of ecstasy pour from us both, reverberating around the chamber.

Being with Luda always feels as if he were designed for me by the Shadowed One themself. The lifetime of demons can feel endless and empty. My life was nothing but a blazing shell of heat and horror before I met the others. Luda brings light to my life. It took a few centuries to acknowledge our feelings. Now that we have, there's no stopping our unbreakable connection. It strengthens with every passing day. My feelings for each member of our unusual group are unique to that specific person. Luda brings me joy and warmth. He can piss me off and irritate me to no end, but he can also make me laugh even when I'm determined to spend the day brooding. He's one of a kind. And he's *mine*.

I drag his torso up, pulling him tightly to my chest, never slowing my pace. His tentacle adjusts, keeping rhythm as it takes me from behind with expert fucking skill. One of my hands grips Luda's throat, the other reaches around to shackle his thick cock. I want to watch, want to feel, want to see the release as it's expelled from his body. His webbed fingers reach above us, ensnaring my horns and making me shudder with unbridled pleasure. He's putty in my hold as I drive into his ass, pump his cock, and tighten my grip around his throat.

My movements stutter as he slides a second tentacle inside me. The two work in tandem, stroking me in all the deep dark places where I so desperately need his lewd affections. A third tentacle grasps my balls, twisting slightly. My horns, my ass, my balls. The stimulation is all too much. I squeeze Luda's throat with the intention of cutting off his air. It's his undoing. I knew it would be.

Luda comes. His body seizes up as he voicelessly cries his release to the castle walls. My eyes are greedy as they watch thick spurts of cum pump out of him and rain down into the water below. I follow him into the release, my cock swelling painfully before releasing my spend deep inside him. Fire burns up my spine and dances across my skin as my climax scorches through me. The world grows hazy, and as my flesh heats, the steam begins rolling off the water once more. Luda's body spasms as it welcomes my cum. His own cock jerks with another, smaller tremor.

I collapse over him, allowing his skin to cool my chest as we both fight for breath. My arm hooks beneath him, supporting his weight as I withdraw from him. His body is limp as I sit back against the ledge and drag him into my arms. Luda is massive in stature, but I'll always be just a few inches taller and broader. He settles into my chest with a contented sigh.

"I love you," Luda murmurs as his tentacles stroke my arms.

Love. Love is a word that didn't exist in our home before Evie. She brought out the best in us and showed us what love truly was. It didn't take long to realize that even though we never said the words, we were all in love. It had always been so much more than a physical attraction between Luda, Reiner, and I. Evie gave us the confidence and security to admit what had been there for so long.

"And I love you, Luda." He relaxes into my hold as I stroke his shoulder. We sit, lost in the steam and silence, simply existing in each other's presence.

"What happened here?"

Luda and I jump to our feet and clamber out of the water. Excitement flares to life within me at the sound of Evie's voice. I flap my wings, clearing the steam and revealing Evie and Reiner.

She slides her eyes along our naked forms. "Whatever it was, I'm jealous I missed it."

Evie's skin is glowing in that soft, lavender way it always does after Reiner's filled her with his electricity. Luda and I exchange a look. The two of us stalk toward Evie, swallowing up the space between us.

"You smell like Reiner," Luda notes as we close in on her. "We'll need to fix that."

"He's had his fun." I grin, revealing my sharp teeth and flicking my tongue out. Evie opens her mouth but I silence her with my hand on her neck. "Now it's our turn."

Thanks for reading!!!

I hope you loved our spooky little Evie and her trio of doting monsters! This has been one of my favorite stories to tell!

Keep going for a sneak peek of *The Wrath of Roses*

What if the Beast took the girl of his dreams AND the man who was desperate to claim her, and used them to act out his every fantasy...

The witch's wrath has left me isolated, broken.

A Beast unable to even touch another living soul without ruining them.

My only solace comes from watching the one I've fallen in love with from afar. *Fleur.*

She's beautiful, spirited, and everything I desire. I can't give her what she needs, but there's one in the village who can...

Gabriel is tall, strong, and handsome—all things I once was. As my days grow lonelier, I accept that I need them —*both* of them.

They'll act out every dark, twisted fantasy my monstrous form prevents me from participating in.

And with any luck, they'll grow to enjoy their new prison.

But the closer we become, the more the roses wither and die. *The castle is changing.* The curse exacts a greater toll each day.

Unless... Is it possible Fleur is meant for more than satiating my most carnal needs?

Could she be the one to break the spell?

Or is it too impossible for anyone to love a Beast?

Contains dark themes including graphic violence, blood, sexually explicit content, dubcon, 18+

Check my website for a full list of content warnings!

The Wrath of Roses: Sneak Peek

"Fleur." A frantic whisper wakes me from my beastly nightmare. What a horrible dream. A shiver skates across my skin as I replay the scenario. Sharp fangs, claw-tipped paws, a frozen dungeon, and cinnamon fur.

"Papa?" Sleep still dusts across my eyes as I take in some light from the room.

"Fleur!" The voice is more forceful this time. Its deep resonance triggers an uncanny familiarity within me.

"Gabriel?" Strong hands grip my shoulders hard enough to hurt. What is he doing in my room? Thick blankets surround my body, their weight keeping me wrapped in a cocoon of warmth and comfort. The velvety-soft fabric glides beneath my fingertips like petals. *This is not my bed.*

A whip of clarity cracks across my mind and I'm wide awake. Gabriel's crystal-blue eyes swim into focus. A loud slap echoes through the room as my hand connects with his chiseled face.

"Fuck." He snatches my wrist in the air and his seething glare makes me freeze. "What was that for?"

"Where have you taken me?" My eyes dart around the space. It's not my home, and it's certainly not Gabriel's. The lack of animal trophies and desperate women make that much abundantly clear.

"I didn't take you anywhere. The Beast took me when I was looking for you. I followed his tracks and attacked him with my men."

"The Beast? That's not possible. It was only a dream."

Gabriel's jaw clenches as he spits the next few words out. "It's very real, Fleur. Look around. We're in the castle."

I do as he says. The room is more spacious than my entire home back in the village. Rich, red, and smooth, gold dominates every wall, piece of furniture, and even the ceiling. The bed we're in is larger than my kitchen. The sumptuous ruby comforter that covers us is decorated with embroidered feather inlays. A snow-white canopy looms above, fastened to the ceiling on a wheel of ornate gold with white plumage around the top. Two gilded angels perch on either corner at the foot of the four-post bed. Their long arms hold the canopy fabric open wide. The center of the bedroom boasts a prodigious chande-lier. Crystal teardrops hang from every inch of the fixture, and tall white candles glow brightly at each peak. The same design is mimicked in the sconces that line the walls.

Several chairs and an impressive wardrobe sit to one side of the bed. Blue and yellow fabrics peek out from beneath one of its closed doors. The last item to draw my attention truly should have been the first. A considerable throne sits across the room. Its high carved back and crimson-lined arms sit in direct alignment with the bed. I've never heard of a throne in a bedroom. Then again, I've never been in a castle.

"Why does he want us?" I wonder aloud.

"I don't know." Gabriel's eyes betray his fear, an emotion I haven't seen from him since we were teenagers.

Every candle in the room extinguishes as the door opens wide, plunging us into darkness. I reach for Gabriel instinctively, gripping his hand so hard his knuckles pop. A dark shadow moves inside. The towering silhouette can barely be seen from the illumination of the candles that line the hall outside our bedroom. Sapphire eyes glow in the inky shadows. *The Beast.*

"Welcome to my home. I will advise you first and foremost not to attempt an escape. If you refuse to cooperate, I'll have no choice but to chain you to the bed. Is that understood?" The voice is deep, and gruff, yet there is something posh and refined about the clipped manner of the words. It's not at all what I expected from a monster.

"Why have you taken us, Beast?" Gabriel is quick to speak. His loud voice makes me jump.

Those luminous blue eyes land on me in the darkness. My body shudders and Gabriel pulls me close. A soft growl comes from the shadows. "I need you. Both of you."

"What for?" I murmur, my curiosity bettering my fear.

"Though I am a monster now, I was once a man...and I have needs that my monstrous form prevents me from fulfilling. The two of you will help satiate my hunger. I will take great pleasure from your pleasure as you act out my every fantasy. Your flesh will be mine to command, your bodies tools to bend to my will. I have watched the village for many years and am certain now that it has to be you, the both of you."

Surely he isn't saying what I think. Our flesh? Our pleasure?

Gabriel's anger fills the room, making the air thick with tension. "Fuck for you? Be your living dolls? Your mind must be as grotesquely twisted as your beastly form. There's nothing you could say to convince me to act out your little fantasies. I'll kill you, and take Fleur back with me, where she belongs, with a man who can give her what she needs."

I tense, preparing for retaliation from the Beast. Instead he chuckles and the sound is far more terrifying than his rage would have been. "That is your final answer? You will not do it?"

Gabriel spits on the floor. "I'd rather die."

The Beast's silence sucks the air from the room. His ocean gaze pins me in its incandescent glow. "And you, Fleur?"

"She's coming with me," Gabriel saves me from answering. The Beast never breaks his gaze. A glimpse of something white breaks through the darkness. Fangs? The Beast is smiling.

"Very well." The candles light as the door swings shut. Was it by magic? Or some sleight-of-hand trick?

"We have to get out of here." Gabriel jumps into action but I remain in the bed, shock seeming to root me to the spot. He roars in frustration when the door won't budge. "There has to be another way out." He continues his search, ripping down curtains and opening every closet and bathroom door in sight. *Why was he smiling?* I sit here, mulling over the question as a bad feeling worms its way into my gut. "Fleur—"

The door to our room opens once more and this time the candles remain lit. The Beast enters, dragging something behind him. His true form is more mountainous and terrible than I remember from last night. Every part of him, from his enormous paws to the curved horns that adorn his head, screams danger. His eyes find mine again and there's a darkness there, a hunger, and I see him in that moment for the true predator he is.

"Let me go!"

"Laurent." Gabriel gasps and I free myself from the Beast's stare, finding a bloodied and battered Laurent at his feet.

Gabriel's right-hand man struggles within the claws of the Beast.

"Where are the rest of my men?" Gabriel demands.

"Dead," the Beast answers dryly. "And he will die too, unless you give me what I want."

"You cannot barter with human life!" shouts Gabriel.

"I can and I will. Have you changed your answer?" The Beast flicks his gaze between us.

"No," Gabriel answers firmly.

The Beast appears disappointed, but unsurprised. "Very well."

Laurent flails violently as the Beast lifts him in the air. One great paw grips the back of his head while he screams.

"Wait!" I start, but it's too late. Laurent's neck snaps with one quick motion before he's dropped to the floor in a heap. A stunned silence fills the room. My mouth hangs open on a scream that never comes. The sound wishes to break free but my air supply is trapped behind a prison of fear.

"Murderer," Gabriel whispers, dropping to his knees. "You killed him."

"I have killed and I will kill again, and again, until you give me the answer I want. Perhaps I'll barter with the old woman next." My heart seizes in my chest. "She's all alone in that house. It wouldn't be hard for me to snatch her in her sleep. Though, the old bat might die of fright before I even get her to the castle."

"No!" My terror spills over, giving me voice. "Please, leave Aida out of this."

"You control what happens to Aida, and the rest of the townsfolk." He strides toward the door, leaving Laurent's body where it fell. "Next time I return, I expect a different answer."

The door slams shut, making the candles flicker. Gabriel rushes to Laurent's body, checking his old friend for signs of life. But I know well that Laurent is dead. His lifeless eyes gaze up at me with the same blank stare I found my father with the morning he passed.

Now all I can think about is Aida, and all the others who have ever been called a friend to Gabriel or me. I can't let them die for me, but can I truly give in to the Beast's demands?

Gabriel's eyes meet mine and I can see the same war raging within his own thoughts. *What are we going to do?*

Also by Violet Taylor

Chosen Shifter Mates Series

A Shifter Fated Mates Paranormal Romance

Frost and Fate

Alpha and Ivy

Lycan and Lark

Country and Clove

Shifter and Seer

Dark Fairy Tale Reimaginings

The Wrath of Roses

Darkly Depraved Monsters

A Collection of Steamy Monster Romance Shorts

Scream for the Scarecrow

Feast of the Vampire King

Frostbitten

Demons and Damiana

A Web of Lust and Sorrow

Ours For Halloween

Stay In Touch

Sign up for Violet's newsletter to keep up with the latest news about books, giveaways, and more!

Connect with Violet Taylor
Official Website - violettaylorauthor.com
Facebook - The Violet Pack
TikTok - @violettaylorauthor
Instagram - @violettaylorauthor

About Violet Taylor

Violet Taylor is a crystal and candle shop owner by day and a paranormal romance novelist by night. She spends her free time fantasizing about living in an isolated mountain cabin with her wonderful husband and herd of fur babies. She prefers her books with magic, mates, and plenty of muscles.